C000015752

TALES C
DISAFFECTED

KEVIN FROMINGS

Edited By Kate Fromings

ISBN: 9798704612117

Contents

HISTORY

Up here is a stillness that I relish. I have always liked these hills. Here the land gently undulates as a relief to the flatter Belgian plain. Maybe you would not call them hills; perhaps 'swellings' would be a better word for you who come from England. A land studded with mountains – or so I was once told. But, to me, they are hills... And I am the one telling this story.

From this shallow depression in the ridge I can look out unseen, and dream my private dreams. In this dell, scooped out of the slope by one of the old battles, prone in the rustling grass, I can listen to the breeze sighing through the clumps of stunted heather. I can gaze down at the little village, nestling like a child's building brick in the folds of a green counterpane.

Did I say that I was invisible to all eyes? All except the jewelled pinheads of the tiny amethyst heather insects that crawl around me. Also perhaps, to the piercing gaze of a soaring hawk as it rides the air currents, searching for a living meal. All I can hear is the quiet roar of the breeze, and the ever-present warbling of skylarks as they revel in the joys of summer... That is why you have caught me here today.

Church and lunchtime have passed, and I have Sunday afternoon all to myself. Maybe I should say 'had' the afternoon all to myself, for you are here now. Did you come on the motor coach that arrived in the village half an hour ago? I saw it all from up here. Some more tourists, I thought, coming to deposit a little rubbish and take away *genuine* relics of the battle.

Are they genuine? Oh, they are *real* enough – hand made in old Pierre's workshop on Friday. Mind you, if the visitors actually showed real intrigue and came up

4

here they would find... But you *are* here. Why? On holiday afternoons I seek refuge in this little hollow, while bored children run about screaming on the hills. They are forever asking if Napoleon or the Kaiser won the battle, and why didn't they have any aeroplanes or tanks?

It is rare for them to encroach on my peace of a Sunday. For that I am thankful... No, no, do not go. You are not disturbing me, as long as you are alone. I did not think anyone would climb the hill today, it is so very hot. You are youthful and strong, obviously. I wonder for how much longer I shall be attracted to this spot, for none of us are getting any younger. I know, sadly, I shall leave it for good one day.

I used to come up here on Sundays to collect any remains of the battle that I could find. It is exciting to uncover a lump of knobbled brown rust in the rough shape of a sword, and then take it carefully to the museum workshop at the back of my humble cottage... You can see it from here actually – the one with the ramshackle roof and overgrown garden. It needs repair, but what can I do in these times?

It was well stocked with souvenirs from the last war... Oh, I apologise. No, 'souvenir' is not perhaps the best word when so many have lost so much... I lost my business, literally. The Boche came and helped themselves. Now it is *their* relics I display. I used to make drawings of the earlier battles. I had a good eye for the colours of the uniforms, but since warfare became all greys and browns I don't have the heart. No one wants Napoleon any more. I suppose, like you, they come for memories of fathers they never knew, or brothers they will never see again.

I tried to write a book about the war once... the ashes of that futile effort have long since been scattered on old Pierre's roses. So, this being Sunday afternoon, I am once again here. Please, do sit down if you wish. No, not there. That is my foot and it cramps me... There? So be it.

I was often told that I had a comfortable lap. The ladies liked to sit on my knee... Well yes, you are right, that is not relevant now. It is, like all other things; past. It is very easy to muddle time here. Your motor coach, for example, could just as easily be a horse drawn charabanc, or a swift barouche; it's all one and the same to me.

Shall I tell you a secret... No, hear me out, I am not rambling. Besides, it may be of some use to you. I am certainly past being able to do anything with it! Up here, hidden by a clump of stunted and twisted hawthorns, there lies a cannon and a whole gun team. Yes, horses and everything!

Well, of course they are just skeletons, but the gun is brass and would look fine in any museum. It would look fine in my own, but I cannot get it there now. Possibly you could help... Ah, there's the catch. I do not exactly remember which tangled thorn-break holds the secret. I thought I'd re-discovered it a couple of years ago; all I did was get careless and silly, and I tripped over a rock. I banged my head and lost my spectacles. Never did find those glasses again...

Anyway, I am drifting. I banged my head... rather hard, you see. Tried to move, but my ankle gave me a jolt of pain. Luckily it was a warm day, and the grass felt so comfortable that I relinquished any idea of trying to get up. Someone would find me in time, or my foot would heal, and it was a pleasant afternoon. No one would forget old Yves. I felt sleepy, and closed my eyes to the drowsy sunshine, cushioned by the sweet heather.

Whether it was the sun that awoke me, or whether it was an animal brushing my face, I was suddenly conscious of a terrific pounding in my head. I do not know how long I had lain insensible to the world, but at first I thought my poor old brain was thumping due to having been broiled in the hot sun. Still, someone would find me soon, for there was smoke drifting across my hiding place. People were obviously burning heather

6

further down towards the village, they would certainly find me.

The thudding grew louder, pummelling my senses like the roar of a passing steam train. There was no pain, just this incredible dull reverberation that almost seemed to be coming from the ground itself, working its way inside my skull. Horses' hooves during a race, I thought sleepily. That thought must have turned the key and unlocked my wits.

There was an explosion of sound. I felt like I was being sucked through a tunnel of whirling images, and I suddenly found myself sitting in the middle of what seemed to be a vast battlefield. The smoke *had* been from burning heather, but no controlled fire this. Hundreds of grey clouds – each with a yellow tail of flame – issued forth from the charred hillside. Every so often the earth would erupt and a new fire would begin. I thought I had entered the furnaces of hell!

Pinching myself hard on the forearm in the vain hope of fleeing this nightmare, I was forced to accept that this was no dream. At first, frozen with terror, I suddenly found that I could move a little, and scrambled to the edge of the hollow to get a better view. I was trying desperately to comprehend what was going on.

Not only had the dip in the ground impaired my field of vision, it had also sheltered my ears from many of the demonic sounds which now assailed them. The monstrous cries were like an infernal concerto. Shouts and screams of frightened, dying, men and horses formed the woodwind section; clattering cannon wheels provided the higher percussion. The strings supplied the hackle-raising screech of metal sliding on metal, as men lunged at each other with bloodied sword and bayonet.

Above it all, so loud that it disappeared into the continuous background of brass and timpani, the heavy bass of the cannons, exploding shot, pounding hooves...

I ducked down with fright every time the earth was rendered. A soldier in a jacket that had once been blue, now stained purple with blood, threw himself down beside me! Feverishly he began to load his musket, and I began to suspect that I was invisible to these people. Therefore – by some divine providence – I was safe to walk out into the chaos completely unharmed. It was a miracle! Luckily I had the chance to put my theory to the test before I had even left my refuge.

Hearing the sound of heavy footsteps, I span around to see the fast approaching figure of an infantryman in a scarlet uniform. His musket was outstretched, and the wickedly long bayonet thrust towards my new companion in the hollow. This stout Frenchman was oblivious to his impending fate, so I reached over and shook him violently, then tried to pull him out of the way. The rough serge of his clothes felt real enough to my touch, yet he totally ignored me – as did his red assailant.

The slithering crunch as the weapon was buried up to the muzzle in his back, the gout of glutinous crimson blood that welled from his mouth and nose to splatter the clean grass in front of him... these awful, awful things will I never forget.

I fled, barely registering that I was safe, whatever happened. All around me I could see thousands of soldiers, some in red coats, some in blue, a few in green. Every once in a while I caught a glimpse of a tall busby belonging to Napoleon's Imperial Guard. Once, I could swear, I snatched a brief view of a tubby little man in a grey coat astride a white horse. The smoke swirled around like autumn mist, and I ran blindly on in the hope that I could escape this madness.

Then out of the vapours came an awesome sight. At first glance it appeared to me as a spectral hearse moving silently across the grass. The cacophony of ball and shot drowned out any individual sound. Then it became more solid: a gun team, driving out at full speed, the horses with their ears flat back to their heads, the riders bending low over their necks. Truly it was a magnificent sight. The leaders swung round, and the whole array bore down on me at a speed that made flight impossible. Like a frightened rabbit I stood until they were so close I could smell the sweat on their skin, and then -

And then I was lying back in this hollow, where you now sit... oh, I see... You have lost interest. They always do, you know. No one wants my stories anymore. If I tell them to the breeze even the wind dies away. But I can't help it; it is dreadfully lonely up here. Whenever someone comes I feel hopeful. When they leave, and the stillness returns I become unsettled. Oh for a moment to spend with Pierre, or my brother Guillaume... Wait, what have you done?

A strange sensation, as if something was clutching my heart, a squeezing deep inside my chest. You have found my glasses at last! Yes, yes, pick them up. Take them back to the village for me. You *do* care. You *were* listening. The others will come now I am sure of it, but by removing part of me you have unlocked the chains that bound me to this beautiful spot.

I have so much to tell you. I have much still to do and see, with your help of course. You wouldn't even know that I was there by your side. But for now we walk down the hill and back to the little village in silence. Merely two companions enjoying the quiet of a midsummer afternoon.

THE SUMMERHOUSE

It was the three hundredth year, an uncelebrated anniversary, forever etched into inanimate objects... yet remembered by no one. Three turbulent centuries had passed. They had seen the summerhouse lying beneath its preserving cover of ivy and creeper. Those two resolute plants that bargain for the privilege of crumbling buildings to the ground in their own time, while holding the weather at bay. Structures were built to last in those days.

A hump of tangled greenery amidst a wilderness of plants once collected and tended by men. Left running to seed so long ago now that they had reverted to their wild strains, centuries before the human line in the manor house was dust and clay. Smaller rises of foliage marked the outlines of the ruined walls of that proud house that had stood strong, in the days of good Queen Bess. Since then it had been made uninhabitable by the careless mishandling of gunpowder, and some errant pipe ashes. All who held ownership of the manor perished... Nature moved in to claim her own.

The grand old lady suffered occasional setbacks. A legal wrangle developed over the property, and continued through several families until the deed of ownership was lost. Last seen fluttering down from the edge of London Bridge during a common street brawl. Then there was the time when a young man had taken refuge from his pursuers by hiding in the half-buried cellars. Armed soldiers had tramped through the gardens, smashing down plants with their heavy boots, slicing through years of carefully placed undergrowth with their swords.

They even attempted to burn the place out, but Nature wasn't going to release her hold that easily. A

10

shower of rain extinguished the flames before their red greed ate up too much vegetation. The fugitive escaped, and to show his gratitude jammed the great gates shut with a thick branch, so that in time they became an extension of the ivy covered walls. No one else should disturb the peace of that hallowed ground which had hidden a true king.

After that time the human race ignored the secluded estate. Politics, wars, pestilence and international crises proved more interesting subjects of concern. The Industrial Revolution passed it by... The densely packed woodland held no allure to the Victorian philanthropists. They were more interested in plucking human fruit from the branches of the looms and mines. Mother Earth built her palace within the high red brick walls that ringed the edge of the land.

The ruins of the summerhouse were soon overrun with creeper, while the ivy – that debt collector amongst vines – began to cover every piece of stone work, growing slowly, but very surely, into a fine mantle over the centuries. For nearly a generation the orchard retained its neat ranks, inevitably rebel fruit trees grew and blossomed from the fallen seeds. A rag tag army of pears, plums and apples marched its all-conquering way across the rose beds. Unperturbed by this intrusion the perfumed thorns wound and twisted their way onto the lawn. That lush expanse of waving grasses, studded in spring with golden daffodils, became pierced in summer by scarlet poppies.

Once neat shrubs and well pruned trees lined oft trodden paths. Now mighty oaks cast their majestic shade over many parts of the gardens, yet not one of these giants could boast of having cooled human skin. The last of the original trees had toppled a century ago, crashing down in a winter gale, smashing onto the old wall as though attempting to break free from its home. Not a brick moved, the thick cushion of ivy tendrils saw to that.

*   *   *

The sun shone gently down on this May morning and caressed the hidden summerhouse with its warm rays. A single shaft of yellow light penetrated the ivy through a ragged hole torn last March by the falling weather vane in a spring gale. The golden beam illuminated the floating motes of dust as they rose and fell – a mist that sparkled with a myriad of tiny diamonds whenever it passed through the bar of daylight.

A summer breeze wandered through the broken window, idly toying with the countless generations of birds' nests that covered the floor. The zephyr whispered through the greening leaves, it spoke of idyllic days yet to come. Delicately the cobwebs wafted, as though trying to clean some of the dust from their densely intricate strands.

A brief shadow flitted across the golden rod; the kestrel plummeted from an azure sky, and snatched at a grey shape on the ground in front of the summerhouse. He flapped lazily to his nest in the clock tower – that crumbling, rotting, place where time had stood still for aeons. He fed the torn mouse to the one mewling, ever-hungry, chick. It wobbled like an animated powder puff in the nest of grass and twigs. This was the latest in a long line of homes to replace the clock face. It was the first to be built when the disc of rusting enamel had finally surrendered to the inevitabilities of the medium it was meant to record.

Wild animals were the only creatures who found their way into the walled enclosure – the diggers and the climbers. Passers-by of a human kind stayed well out in the road, intent on making their way to the nearest inn. There was nothing here for them. No grand historic structure or shaded ruin in which to picnic. Just an impenetrable mass of vicious brambles, ivy and ferocious jagged nettles.

Not all the house had succumbed to the fateful gunpowder cocktail. One wing had stood, albeit roofless, until as recently as the last war. A smoking Heinkel bomber had roared down, a victim of one of the many aerial duels in the dangerously clear skies of 1940. An iron bird smashing a precarious ruin to make a final nest of bricks for itself. Even this modern intruder hadn't been spared the attentions of the determined ivy. Severe lines of twisted and buckled aluminium were now a mass of tough green stalks.

The birds and animals utilised this fallen warrior. Several generations of field mice lived in various nooks and crannies, while a flame-breasted family of robins had found refuge in the remains of the empty skull of the pilot.

*   *   *

The walker ceased writing, and glanced across at the ancient book which lay open on the grass beside him. He tried to imagine this wild British jungle as the neat gardens portrayed on the yellowing page. Narrowing his eyes, he attempted to recreate the fine Tudor architecture. Nature had been the grounds keeper for far too long. The picture in the book might just as well have come from a fairy tale; it bore no relation to reality.

He stood up, and ran his hand over the low moss-covered stone set into the gatepost. His fingertips tried to pick out the worn, carved letters. They were illegible, ending up as just so many bumps and dents in the green velvet surface. Instead, he read the inscription through as it was noted in the book he had acquired:

13

Oh to be at Windhovere
Now that sumer is heere,
To smell the newe mown clover,
The hopps to mak the beere,
To see the hunteres riding after
The swifte foote deere,
To be close with the familie,
To knowe that friends are nere.

The walker closed the ancient tome and allowed himself a smile. He felt a sudden close affinity with that long-dead sentimentalist. Flicking open a business-like jotter to a page marked 'Prospective Sites', he drew a line through the word 'Windhovers'. Then, with a slight shrug of his young shoulders, he packed the remains of his sandwiches into his rucksack. He took a farewell peek through the ivy-bound gates to where the summerhouse must have been, and trudged off in the direction of the nearby village.

The kestrel soared into the sky, and hovered on the gentle breeze, revelling in the sultry afternoon air. The single shaft of sunlight disappeared from the summerhouse instantly, as if it had been switched off. Phaeton's fiery chariot moved on across a cobalt sky. It would forever return, as sure as the summerhouse would always be there to receive it.

SENSE OF PURPOSE

Once more his mind wandered away from his body. Like a piece of India rubber. Just as it reached the point where he thought it would snap and break free it would catapult back again. At the furthest position he would find himself looking down on the shape that was himself with a dispassion born of forgetfulness. Whenever the two entities – mental and physical – were forced together, the intense pain severed them almost instantly.

His spirit was already atop the steep scarp of Holly Hill; it was already standing amongst the wiry tufts of grass that would be bowing and dancing in the evening breeze... Black flocks of birds would be scarring the crimson horizon as they returned to their evening roost in the forest which covered the ridge at his back. The early mists would be creeping over the dusk-purpled landscape. An unequal draughtboard of fields; southern England in all its eighteenth century glory.

The body lagged agonisingly behind the mind. His once powerful legs - "Oi seen 'im run two moile without a thought" - staggered from side to side. They were carrying a heavily sagging torso that threatened to overbalance them at every step. Sometimes he swayed off the road, barging into the bushes and brambles that lined the edge of the wooded banks. Thorns tore at his clothes and slashed at his pallid skin. Older blood had long since soaked his shirt... He witnessed it splashing onto the sun-baked chalk beneath him in a thick red spatter.

If he'd been able to look back (an impossibility now if he had any hope of carrying on), he would have seen the rich scarlet liquid soak into the white dust and fade to a rusty orange brown.

Three miles he had run, then staggered, and was even now crawling, supporting himself on flesh-raw hands and knees. That pain was blotted out by the greater torture engulfing his body. The pistol balls had missed him completely in the hectic melee of frightened men and jostling horses, but the sabre had sliced a diagonal gash across his chest. A silvery sword, sharp as a razor, quick as lightning. Such an odd sensation as it had parted his flesh and bitten deep across the bone.

He had watched, fascinated, as his own blood sprayed out, painting the glinting steel in moist scarlet. His legs half buckled under him in the moment, then recovered, and he ran... and ran...

Again he fell. He knew that this time he wouldn't be able to even raise himself to his knees. Without pausing, he floundered through the dust like a fish out of water. A fish desperately panicking as it tried to edge itself back to its own watery world before the final blow of the fisherman's club. His sight suddenly dimmed, and he thought it was the bitter end until he realised that this stretch of the road had fallen into a premature twilight, shadowed by the surrounding beech trees.

Would he make it in time? It was the first occasion that the thought had entered his agonised brain. As he became aware that he might fail, the strength seemed to fly from his body. *Of course he would achieve his goal!* Why would he have survived for so long if God had not meant it to be so! Returning faith in the task at hand brought increased energy. The bloody flesh that had until recently been sturdy muscular limbs scrabbled once more on the unyielding chalk track; a valiant effort to move his body forward. The arid dust billowed up in lazy white clouds from beneath his clutching hands, while dirt, sweat, and blood mingled in a sticky wine-red preparatory sacrament. On the other road in the valley below, invisible still to his tear-blinded eyes, his companions would be approaching. *They must be warned.* He could look to his own condition later. *He must give them the signal.*

Quickly he struggled up a cowslip-strewn bank, staggering back several times before he was over the top... and then there was the unexpected gate. Blood, now fresh, dripped and mingled with the dainty yellow flowers creating a sunset of a life... a palette echoed in nature. Was it his mind wandering again? No, a wave of exquisite pain washed over him, sobering him enough to see through the mist of bodily fluids that the wooden gate really *was* there.

Somehow he had reached it, but he remained unaware of how, or what the cost in strength had been. Arms that should have no power in them hauled his mangled frame up so that he was draped over the timber like the carcase of a hunted stag. Raw stumps of fingers fumbled with the metal latch, his nails mere ribbons of skin. He fell through the opening, rolled down the other bank, and on to the sweet summer grass, damp, pungent from an early dew.

For a moment he lay still. Waves of darkness washed over him, yet he fought to stay conscious. The last rays of the setting sun were eagerly soaked up by his shivering body, giving his death-pallored skin an almost healthy tint. He raised his eyes skywards. Through the singing in his ears came another music, more liquid, spreading life and joy. He couldn't see the lark, but it was enough to know that the small bird was there close by, encouraging him to keep on. Then the song mingled with a harsher sound; hooves pounding on the dusty soil of the chalk road above, behind him.

Focussing his eyes as much as they would on the Pilgrim's Way, half obscured by verdant summer foliage a hundred feet below, he saw men and laden donkeys. They were bursting into flowers of moving vermilion and mauve as they made their slow way forward, disappearing every time they ambled behind leafy trees and bushes, of which there were plenty lining the narrow lane. All of a sudden a solitary pistol cracked behind him, but the ball went wide, and buried itself in a low hanging rowan branch.

With supernatural effort, lifted by the waning sun and an overwhelming fear for his friends, he suddenly leapt to his feet. Like a whale breaking water he raised his arms to the flaming auburn sky, and expelled the last of the air from his lungs in a final desperate shout.

"*A trap! It's a trap! Be gone!*" The convoy on the Pilgrim's Way sprang into animated life, scattered, and melted into the rural landscape, just as the riders on the hill came into view.

The Revenue men reigned in their horses, and watched with a sickened satisfaction after the shout, as his blood soaked body lurched forward in a grotesque cartwheel, rolling limply down the steep hillside, just like a puppet suddenly cut from its strings. Their smiles soon turned to curses, as they realised that the lane below was now deserted.

They couldn't walk their skittish horses down the sharp slope ahead. The only way for them was to go back by the road they had come on, and that would take a full ten minutes; ample time for the people, like pack animals, to disperse. For the sake of one corpse they'd lost a whole train of contraband. Sullenly they wheeled round and ambled back to the open gate. Thence to the road, their hoof beats receding hollowly in the twilight.

He now stood quietly at the top of Holly Hill, having entered into the blessed transition.

He bathed his weary mind in the last single view of the full and glorious sunset. It stretched out across the endless landscape. With a pitying, but detached, glance he focussed on the crumpled shape that lay hunched in the grass below, clothes slick with blood, its hair a matted mess. He let his senses float free...

They reached ever upward to a clear blue infinity, and as he closed his eyes, at last he was at peace.

THE POACHER

With the wind singing cheerfully through the bracing wires, the smart new De Havilland 4 flung itself around the blinding bright sky of a British summer. Visible for miles around, the taught cream canvas stood out against the cerulean infinity, occasionally hiccuping little puffs of black smoke as the engine revved during a steep climb. From the ground below, the sound ebbed and flowed on the gentle breeze, an agitated insect that would not settle.

The pilot, strapped into the front cockpit, let out great whoops of excitement as he dipped, turned, and banked the aircraft. He sent it wheeling, tumbling over the green woods and fields of Kent. Imprisoned – his word for it – in the seat behind, was a passenger who was feeling anything but excited. The gyrations of the flying machine turned his stomach. He gripped the leather rimmed sides of the cockpit with white knuckles.

"Christ, don't let me fall out..." he muttered through gritted teeth, lips purple with cold.

"I told you it was fun!" cried his friend, as the aeroplane screamed into a dive over a long strip of open grassland. It scattered small birds and rabbits who had nervously hopped out into the warm sun for a brief siesta.

A poacher, robbed of his game, threw himself face down in the grass as the machine beat up the field. He swore vehemently as he realised that a herd of cows had only recently vacated the meadow. Lifting himself up from the sticky brown mess, he furiously turned his gaze skyward, just in time to see the De Havilland climb again above the short hawthorn hedge bordering the neighbouring field. It was banking round in preparation for a repeat performance.

"Don't do it!" yelled the passenger in the rear, not realising that his words were being whipped away by the icy blast of the slipstream.

Enraged, the poacher stuffed two cartridges into his shotgun, slammed the barrels shut, and then waited for the great raucous bird to whoosh in another low pass along the turf. This time he stood his ground, crouching instinctively at the last moment, missing the landing gear by mere feet. When the aircraft was overhead he angrily discharged both barrels into the flimsy framework of wood and canvas, the unexpected recoil from the gun throwing him forcefully onto his back.

"That'll teach the stupid bastards..." he grumbled vindictively as he followed the path of the low-flying menace with watery eyes.

Above in the aircraft the pilot slumped sideways, one dead arm trailing over the side of the cockpit. His head lolled drunkenly, eyes glazed over, left to stare through the ragged hole in the bottom of the plane. Helplessly his friend fumbled with his own straps, terrified of what he knew was to come. His heart raced with alarm even though everything seemed suddenly to be moving in a sluggish haze.

Lifting himself up from the ground on to one elbow the poacher saw the aeroplane rise slightly, then fly straight and level. It made no attempt to pull up above the tall leafy barrier of oak trees that stood guard at the end of the meadow. He saw both wings rip off like paper around a matchstick model. The red hot engine exploded impressively as it smashed into a solid tree trunk. It ripped away from the fuselage, scattering burning fuel onto the scrub below. Amid the hissing of the flames a pheasant screeched, and the poacher cursed again.

Reaching into his pocket, unable to drag his eyes away from the fireball, he fumbled two more cartridges into the gun and stood up. Carefully, yet still slightly stunned by the speed of events, he began to walk forward.

If anyone had survived that crash, he was going to make damned sure that it wouldn't be for long. They could identify him. They could stand in the dock and say "aye m'lud it was him that shot us down over Camberly's field". They could have him banged up again, for more than just thieving a coney or two...

Fifteen feet above the nettle strewn ground, acrid smoke drifting around it, the broken fuselage lay on its side. It was lodged between two sturdy branches. The dead pilot hung forward in his seat straps, like a discarded marionette. The stricken passenger became aware that he was conscious, but had no recognition of waking up. Something slid across his forehead, tickling the skin, and then moved down the side of his nose into his mouth. The warm salty taste seemed almost comforting... Still with his eyes closed, he slowly moved his hand to touch his head.

A thin, razor precise, horizontal gash above his eyebrows oozed blood that ran down his face forming a revolting crimson mask. He moved his head to stop the stinging torrent running directly into his eyes, and carefully opened them. Reaching out, he prodded his friend in the back. Even in his groggy state he realised that the pilot was either dead, or severely wounded. He must get help, and after that he was going to give his friend a *very* stiff talking to, broken bones or not... No, that wasn't right. His dazed mind was playing tricks. He would simply decline their next outing politely, and spend the weekend playing bridge with his cousins over in Sevenoaks... By God, why was it so hard to concentrate?

With great difficulty he managed to delve around in his coat pocket until his fingers closed around the hard form of a very sharp pocket knife. This he managed to open, and he sawed unsteadily at his leather safety harness until it gave way, sending him crashing to the hard ground below.

Hearing the noise from the far edge of the field, the poacher froze in mid stride. His mouth tightened in a frown of determination as he raised the shaking shotgun to his shoulder. What had he done? Well, he had let his anger get the better of him as usual, that's what his wife would say if he ever told her... Now look at this mess... Squinting down the barrels, he pointed the gun at the gap in the trees where he knew any survivor of the crash would emerge. At this range he couldn't miss, and for a moment he hesitated. What *was* he thinking?

Yes, he was already a minor criminal – had been poaching his whole life, had several custodial sentences under his belt to prove it – but murder? For that's what it would be: premeditated, or some such fanciful law term, cold blooded murder. These weren't animals for the pot, they were people. Well, sod it, those flying men should have thought of that when they tried to put the wind up him. They should have thought about the food they scared away; things were tight enough as it was!

Right on cue, there was a crackle of dry undergrowth, and the expected figure appeared. The recognisable uniform took the poacher a bit off guard. Had he interrupted a military training session? He swallowed his mounting nerves. The army did occasionally use the countryside hereabouts, but on a Sunday afternoon didn't they? Not on a Saturday morning, so early that the dew was still wet on the fields...

The soldier was limping, his face bathed in dark claret, from which two startlingly white eyes stared fixedly at the poacher. The right arm was raised, not dramatically, but rather like an orchestral conductor signalling the start of a symphony. Instead of a baton, the gloved fingers were clutching a large, open, pocket knife. The soldier didn't speak; slowly, surely, he moved forward.

Smoothly, almost leisurely, the cornered poacher aimed and pulled the trigger. His finger felt strong, unwavering against the metal. He was now certain this was the only way. The right hand barrel discharged its contents into the advancing soldier's chest, making it look as though someone had thrown a pot of red paint over his already stained khaki uniform. Thrown backward by the sudden impact, the injured military man staggered, yet soon regained his balance. He came on just as confidently, still in total silence.

The poacher emptied the other barrel, less sure of himself now. He watched in morbid fascination, as everything aligned in his mind. A gaping hole appeared where once a strong neck had been. The uniform was now so soaked in blood that no other colour was to be seen; it took on the look of a purple undertaker's funeral suit... And still the man came forward, his single arm raised, his eyes two searing white dots in a lake of red.

Scrabbling in his shirt pocket for fresh cartridges, the poacher backed off, hurriedly reloading. Again he fired, both barrels this time from the hip. It threw his balance, and the gun nearly twisted out of his hands as he stumbled on the uneven clumps of grass. Luckily the shots went home.

He wanted to turn and run. At the pace the soldier was coming he could easily get away, but something told him that wherever he fled to it wouldn't be far enough. This quarry was not going to die quietly. This quarry was not going to *die*.

Trees now surrounded him on three sides. He had been backed into the opposite end of the meadow from the crash site. On the last shot the creature, now with the side of his head blown out, was oozing a whitish pulp that mingled with the blood. Still the small pocket-knife flashed in the sun. The poacher stared at it, hypnotised, unable to break away. If only he could shoot at that outstretched arm... His hands now shook so much that he lost valuable seconds in trying to reload the barrels, almost dropping his last two cartridges.

As the bloodied thing came closer, the poacher could hear a rasping, gurgling sound. It was regular, like someone breathing through a heavy bout of bronchitis. Occasional puce coloured bubbles would swell from between the flayed lips, and then burst, leaving a fine bloody mist on the air.

The poacher's eyes were wide with a terror that bordered on madness, he began to laugh, nervously – hysterically. He felt the cold steel of the barrels on his chin, digging into the flesh as they moved in his terrified hands. Something – *anything* – to take away that horrific sight… The mouth of the soldier opened, strings of scarlet saliva hanging from cream teeth, like prison bars to a dark formidable cave, his outstretched arm was almost touching the poacher's heaving chest.

And with that, the terrorised man pulled both triggers.

*   *   *

Two plain-clothed members of the local constabulary stood in the middle of the field. Yesterday's sunshine had turned to a soaking drizzle. They were trying to compare notes, and keep their papers dry at the same time. They were failing.

"What I can't understand," said one, "is why that poor bloke with the shotgun didn't go and get help. After all, a crash is a crash, even if you've got your mind set on committing suicide."

"Haven't you looked at the wreckage?" asked his partner.

"No, I was tied up with that chap who found them. The farmer, I believe. Bit of a nervy mess I can tell you. Three bodies all in one go. can't have been easy to see."

"The aeroplane body has signs of shotgun damage; the pilot too, right through the cockpit… although he may have ultimately been killed in the crash. Won't be able to tell until the autopsy." They both looked

25

towards the sagging wreckage in the tree. "Anyone else in the aircraft?" His colleague checked his scribbled statement, already smudged from the damp.

"Yes, a male passenger," He flicked through the notepad. "Now, he must have really panicked we think. Seems he cut his own straps, fell right out after the plane got lodged in the trees; broke his neck when he hit the ground. Found him lying just below the pilot, poor devil. Would have died instantly."

DUNCAN'S BLUFF

Duncan turned, panting for his life's breath. He staggered backwards, tripping over tough heather roots that clutched at his legs like strong skeletal hands. Time and again he almost fell, but luck, and an inbred intimacy with the highland terrain, kept him running. Again he lumbered backward into a patch of bracken, wanting to see his pursuers but not wishing to halt.

A grouse whirred noisily from under his feet, squawking with rage and fright. The sound echoed out across the valley, carried by the wind until it beat upon the grey rocks that edged the loch half a mile away. One of the red coated soldiers looked up and pointed at the terrified clan elder. The others let out a whoop of glee and began to move through the heather once more, and up the steep side of the foothill.

Summoning his last reserves of strength, the weary Scot forced himself to scramble ever higher, making for the top of the mountain in the manner of a trapped hare that makes for the middle of the field at harvest time. Seeing the prey moving again, a British soldier dropped onto one knee and raised his weighty musket to his shoulder. His companions followed his example. Duncan winced as the sharp crack of the report exploded onto his ears. Weaponry used singly over a long distance was inclined to be hopelessly inaccurate, but the British army of 1745 relied on their vast numbers more than sharpshooting skill. Thus it was that Duncan felt the lead ball rip into the soft flesh of his thigh.

Terror rather than pain flashed into his panic-stricken mind as his leg gave way beneath him and he collapsed into the muddy sludge of a peat bog. Dazzling white stars burst before his eyes and he tensed, waiting for the thud of heavy boots to be followed by the merciless stab of a cold bayonet. His moment had come. A shout of triumph on the moor below changed to one of fright, and the highlander rolled over in an effort to view this welcome turn of events. His blurry eyes were at first only able to focus on the waters of the loch, and the heather-purpled hills beyond, but slowly he worked his way up from the shingled shore, across the lower grass slopes and finally rested his gaze on a pale patch of lime green – the mossy surface of an active marsh.

One of the braver redcoats had suddenly found himself up to the waist in the clinging mire. Others buzzed around him like agitated midges. Duncan grinned humourlessly as the Sassenachs rushed to their friend's aid, retreating again when they found the ground unsafe to support their sixty-odd pounds of equipment. A hurried shouting match ensued, which resulted in the stricken soldier surrendering his pack to the mud and wading backwards until his comrades could drag him onto more solid ground.

A few well chosen curses battered the air as the hunters realised that their prize was now hidden from view. Duncan prayed that this would make them lose heart and return to the loch. He looked up the hill, and realised that what he had taken for his own drenching sweat was a soaking drizzle filtering down from the sodden sky. It seemed to grow lower by the minute, threatening to crush the earth beneath its dark swirling mass. Lying still, he was hidden from below by a belt of shrivelling dead bracken. He was safe, until the Sassenachs began their advance once more. They would not return to the loch without proof of his demise. It would surely be against orders.

He desperately scanned the land above him, searching for a hiding place, secretly knowing that it would be useless. there were no caves in these parts, and the thin birch trees were few. Then his tired eyes alighted on a slight hummock; a man-made mound that had been raised thousands of years before by the ancestors of his ancestors. It was on the edge of the marsh, a difficult place to reach for his enemy. Not really knowing why – almost past caring what happened to him – he dragged his wretched body through the rough, cutting, bracken. His mud-stained jacket and plaid that was once the envy of many officers in the Pretender's army was ripped and torn by the relentless tough heather. His hands grew raw and bloody as he grabbed at anything that would take his weight. He hauled his injured carcass across the seemingly endless yards of hillside.

At last he reached the burial mound, and a dull relief flooded his whole being. In his haste to flee from the barbarous gang of Sassenachs, his bewildered mind had brought him back to the hills and playgrounds of his childhood. Possibly his subconscious had known of the mound's existence the whole time. After all, it was the burial place of a great chieftain whose bones had long since powdered into dust. The portal stone had been removed by Cromwell's soldiers a century before, but Duncan knew none of this. He merely eased his battered limbs into the dim unnatural interior and allowed his mind to succumb to a greater darkness...

*　　　*　　　*

The job of flushing out fugitive rebels was a slow process, but very necessary – according to the orders of the Duke of Cumberland. Thus the patrol of nine British soldiers found themselves in full pack advancing over innocent looking hills that were proving to be just as treacherous as the natives. Beautiful in hot weather, the landscape was nevertheless dotted with deep ravines and sucking marshes. Scotch mists could suddenly descend and instil a chill dampness in bodies that took more than a ration of grog to dispel. Already irked by the rain, cold, and general dismal conditions of their purge, the patrol cursed their superiors.

When they found themselves confronted by a fast-flowing river they also cursed God, and anything else that came into their weary brains. Normally shallow and easy to cross in two strides, the stream was swollen by the rain. It foamed down the hillside as if to say "turn back enemies of my land. You shall not pass!" Not one trooper failed to fall beneath the ice cold waters as they waded across the boulders, their equipment trying to drag them to the shingle bottom for ever. Each swore angrily on the far bank when he found that his powder was soaking.

Slowly they realised their new predicament: they were cut off in an alien and hostile country – aggressors without their means of aggression. All they had were their bayonets for protection. Corporal Dyke, the unloved leader of the patrol, spotted the burial mound further up the hillside beyond the bracken and bog. He grinned lopsidedly. Some entertainment was needed to take their minds off this awkward state of affairs.

"'Ere lads, let's peg that barbarian you shot out on that grass hummock as a warning. Crowell be down in no time for 'is eyes!" Private DeWolfe shivered with something other than cold.

"Are you trying to be amusin'? That's one of them '*aunted mounds*. Even the Scotch blokes don't go near 'em." The corporal laughed, then spat. But when he spoke again a hint of nervousness had crept into his voice.

"Huh, you're just too bloody superstitious. Must be the mountains gettin' to your brains. I'm goin' to do it, and I order you lot to help – no excuses!"

One or two muttered complaints were heard. Dyker had been worried about this bunch from the moment he'd been put in charge of them... lazy collection of idle slackers!

"Oi! You men; just stop your bloody moaning and carry on will you. I don't like askin' twice!" He stomped off. More for effect than anything else he commenced to slash at the tangled bracken fronds with his bayonet. Seeing that there was no avoiding this chore the others followed his example, albeit half-heartedly.

Their meagre search brought them very quickly to the elevated grave site, and they flung themselves down on the grassy hillock, exhausted, drizzle soaked, and very apprehensive. Dusk was falling, and with it the rain was giving way to a thick, eerie, mist. No one spoke. Several men were shivering, particularly when they gazed towards the loch and saw the twinkle of warm camp fires and lanterns. The tents and hot food seemed a thousand miles away. They hadn't even found the body, though they knew he had fallen round about.

"See," said Dyker eventually, sensing that he had to break the uneasy silence. "It's just an 'ill. A knoll. A lump of bleedin' wet grass in the middle of a bleedin' wet country. It ain't haunted. You're just too bloody -" A horrendous moan rent the air, cutting him off in mid sentence. A truly soul-chilling groan that seemed to issue from the very soil beneath his feet. Every one stood up at once. Dyker dropped his musket, and his mouth fell open in a mixture of disbelief and dread. The weapon rolled away into the grasses at the base of the mound.

"W-what was that," someone eventually whispered. The men began to shake.

"Just the wind," replied Dyker in a voice that appeared to have risen two octaves. One of the redcoats had meanwhile discovered the entrance to the chamber.

"But it came from in here," he said, backing away. As if in confirmation of his statement another terrible cry assailed their ears, and sent the dispirited soldiers, into a frightened huddle as far from the opening as they could get without falling into the marsh behind them. Dyker made certain that he was the centre of the group.

31

"Come on, lads, be cautious now," he stammered. "Let's get away from this place. There could be a dangerous animal in there: a wolf, a possessed hound, or a bear..."

"There ain't no bears no more," said DeWolfe, always wanting the last word, "It's... ghosts! Spectres!"

"Well, I ain't waitin' to find out what it is! We shall make what I'll report as a 'tactical withdrawal'." Dyker was not interested in last words; he merely wanted to save face and be gone from that place as quickly as was possible without actually 'running away.'

Alas, even running was near impossible as the mist had caused them to lose their uncertain bearings. No more could they see the friendly camp, or the beach at the edge of the loch. They trudged on up the hillside, cold and wet, looking for a place to bivouac which would give them a good vantage point when the sun rose.

*　　*　　*

His eyes flicked open and registered the same darkness. What had awakened him? Was it the wound, or the fearful groans that he was vaguely aware had issued from his own mouth while he lay semi-unconscious? Dull pain throbbed in waves across his leg, and he felt powerless to move; a man in an agonised nightmare, a prisoner of this endless, fearful, subterranean night. Although his joints were locked in a vice of cold, he rolled over onto his back, and slipped once more into an exhausted oblivion.

Fitful visions of screaming highlanders ran through his dreams – men on a bleak moor, herding like cattle before a line of red coated Englishmen. The whistle of shot as it scythed into the brave clansmen. The charge... then he was home, snuggled up in a blanket before a roaring log fire, the sound of a storm whistling round the ramparts of his family stronghold... Outside the swirling vapours wrapped themselves even tighter around the ancient burial mound, as though trying to protect the inmate from prying eyes.

It was three days before the mountains threw off their misty garments, allowing the heathered slopes to bathe their sweet purple flowers in warm morning sunlight. A golden ray filtered through the portal of the tumulus and caught Duncan full in the face, as if it was cradling him in a warm fleece and dry clothes. He awoke gently, no longer freezing or afraid; just rested, and very hungry.

When he moved, an indistinct pain in his leg caused him to open his eyes. Suddenly it all came back to him – the chase, the mad scramble for safety, his wound. The delicious feeling of being in a sun-warmed cocoon deserted him, and he once again felt bruised and chilled. Carefully he eased himself into a sitting position and studied the hole in his thigh. The flesh around the wound was still tender and pink; although untreated, the gash was clean, healing slowly. He tried to wrap his once proud plaid around himself, but found that the mud soaked cloth had set in the position he had slept in.

Dragging himself to the doorway, and brighter light, he was able to examine his shoddy appearance in more detail. His elegantly tailored jacket (the royal red one that he had seen in Inverary, its gold braid almost glowing), was nothing more than a buttonless rag! The left sleeve was hanging on a gorse bush somewhere near Culloden. The elegant buckled shoes lay at the bottom of a deep river south of Glencoe. Royal Stewart had been the tartan of his plaid, but the muck had reduced it to the dirty brown tones of the Hunting Stewart.

Hunting Stewart: how ironic, he thought sourly. Here he was wearing the colours of the gamekeeper, yet he was the prey. Yawning, he rubbed his hand across his face and felt the stubble which pricked his once clean-shaven chin. All his old standards lay, like the standard of

33

the Pretender, on the trampled grass of the battlefield. A great bubble of regret and longing welled up inside him as he remembered the razor sharp claymore that he had left buried in the stomach of the first chieftain who had tried to flee the field – Duncan's hasty action had been the last throw of a gambling idealist; when he found himself weaponless he too had had to run, and once the panic had exploded inside him it controlled his complete being.

Every step away from the field of Culloden was a step further away from all the things that he had stood for: loyalty of the clans, justice for people in their own land, the need to fight to the death in support of your beliefs. All these had been swept away by fear; fear of a shaft of steel fifteen inches long... a bayonet controlled by a murdering Sassenach. Curse his foolish pride and stupid cowardice! Without his sword he was helpless. He had no defence and no means of snaring any food, and it was food that was his prime concern; not having eaten for four days was playing tricks on his senses, he was sure of it.

Hauling himself to the top of the mound, Duncan gazed enviously at the cluster of tents down by the loch. The little red coated figures down there must have breakfasted well for it was a base camp, stocked with provisions, mainly edible he assumed. He belched involuntarily at the thought of a warm bowl of oatmeal, and felt the pains of hunger even more acutely.

The sound of a rushing burn close by gave him an idea. He remembered a day back in his childhood, a day that had lasted a whole summer, when his friend had taken him to a local stream to tickle for trout. The noble clan chieftain found it very difficult at first, but Iain McGowall, son of a humble crofter, had been exceedingly patient with his pupil. Iain... what had become of him? Duncan had last seen him waving his claymore above his head and charging with those Campbells who had remained loyal to the Pretender. When the survivors had straggled back McGowall was not amongst them...

The burn certainly looked promising, but he could only reach it by the slow process of dragging himself through the coarse heather, unless... glancing around for a suitable crutch, his eyes alighted on a soaked, slightly rusting musket at the base of the burial mound. Little did he know that it had been discarded by the corporal Dyker in the rush to escape. The perfect implement! He hauled himself onto his good leg and collapsed as a wave of bruised pain flooded his body – he'd clearly suffered more than he thought.

As he lay there a thought came into his head. A thought so obvious that he cursed himself for a fool! Here he was on an open hillside, wanted by the British army purely so that they could have the pleasure of killing him, and all he could think about was food. He had to run, and run, he had no time to think of a hot meal and clean clothes, and... his stomach immediately sent a message for sustenance that quelled the panic in his mind. It was as if all else had been silenced and he knew only of that primal need for food. He became a brave leader once more – if he was going to die, then he was definitely not going to die hungry or begging on his knees.

Once again he stood up, only this time he forced his complaining limbs to hobble over to the burn. Water gushed and trickled through the polished rocks, moving down the mountain foothills in a succession of deep, clear, pools and foaming white waterfalls. Finally it emptied into the loch at the very spot where the red coats had placed their camp. Bronze spotted fish glided amongst the stones and weed, then darted for cover as a filthy, unkempt, face invaded their private domain. Brown trout! Praise be!

Duncan gulped down the fresh water, and welcomed the slightly light-headed feeling that he felt as the icy liquid soothed his empty stomach. After several minutes of delightful slobbering he raised his head, allowing water droplets to run down his chin and chest in a cascade now made of jewels by the bright sun. Tiny streams of liquid fire ran down his arms, and he laughed. No one could kill him on such a perfect morning as this!

He crawled to another, as yet undisturbed pool, and carefully put his right hand into the water. Slowly, and very gently, he wiggled the fingers; a new alien pondweed offering shelter to an unsuspecting young trout. One of these denizens of the pool gingerly approached, seemingly hypnotised by the movement it edged even closer... a sharp flick of the wrist and a glistening missile somersaulted onto the grass. A sharp bang with a stone halted its agonised flapping, and the fingers once again began wafting below the water.

Catching the three fish had done much to boost the young man's confidence. He looked at his breakfast, and – despite his hunger – knew that he'd never be able to eat them raw. Tinder was plentiful so he soon had the makings of a good campfire, save for one important item: he had lost his tinderbox days ago. Depressed, he once more looked to the loch, and thought again of Iain McGowall. Even he wouldn't have been able to solve this new problem... While he pondered, his hands absent-mindedly toyed with the firing mechanism of the musket. The flint snapped over, bruising his thumb... Yes! He had a flint - no powder though, which would have helped.

He pressed the trigger several times, and watched the sparks fly from the firing pan. God, if only his highlanders had procured more weapons like this, then it would have been a different fight. He placed the musket beside his dried bracken, and soon a tidy little fire was burning under the three mouth-watering trout that sizzled expectantly on a birch twig spit. His ravenous hunger had made him careless. A pale stream of blue smoke made its way up into the sky, blown into eventual invisibility by the morning breeze.

*   *   *

Corporal Dyker noticed the thin wisp of smoke, and quickened his angry pace towards the burial mound. Had another patrol already arrived and found his musket? For three days he and his men had taken shelter in that damned mist on the hillside. Having to share a hastily cobbled-together den under a rocky outcrop, with men he disliked was *not* made better by the discovery that he had lost his only weapon. If his commanding officer found out he'd be skinned alive. The chance that a rebel was even now killing a soldier with it flashed horribly through Dyker's sullen brain. Still, at least the mist had cleared and some other bugger had probably found the weapon first, thinking it a great treasure.

Deciding that he might as well get it over with, Dyker changed direction, heading for the fire. It was surely a local shepherd or hermit cooking their morning's fare, getting ready for a harsh day ahead. He strode out, keeping his eye fixed on the dwindling smoke signal. As he passed through a stand of wind-beaten birches and gorse he saw Duncan at the same moment as Duncan looked up from the flames! Both tensed, and then relaxed again, as each realised the others predicament. Seeing that the redcoat was unarmed, the Scot tried a desperate bluff; he was unable to run, and he wanted to finish off his man before more help could be summoned.

Even as he was drawing the vicious bayonet from its scabbard Dyker saw Duncan raise the musket to his shoulder. He froze, a half smile locked on his lips. As a British soldier he was the tough 'bully' to his men, but like most tormentors, he was too fond of his own skin to risk charging at a man with a gun. In his weary state he had totally forgotten that the musket was unloaded, and assumed the worst. Dyker stood, uncertain, wondering what he should do.

"Come here, Sassenach," called Duncan, surprised at the sound of his own voice; it had been days since he'd spoken to anyone other than himself. The tone was hoarse. You sound old, he thought, old and worn out with life – let's hope he doesn't recognise the tone.

"The man's a fool," thought Dyker, "He's plenty lean – and wounded by the look of him – once I get close, that's it. He'll be no more." So slowly he walked to the river bank, his bayonet loose in the scabbard – one deft arm movement and a throat could be cut. As he moved closer he could see the open wound on Duncan's leg. He grinned inwardly, and continued walking forward. Before he had a chance to put any plan into action, Duncan played his hand. He jabbed the barrel of the musket into the redcoat's groin!

As Dyker doubled up with the excruciating pain, winded by the blow, Duncan swung the butt up hard into his face! The English soldier, his jaw surely broken, collapsed unconscious at his enemy's feet.

"That's how it should ever be," muttered the Laird, thankful that he had gained enough strength to carry out the risky attack.

*   *   *

It was only an hour later that Dyker's patrol came down the hill to look for him. They were cold, hungry for some grog, and all had weeping blisters from the wet leather of their boots. Two men had streaming colds and one had the beginnings of a bad attack of pneumonia. Dyker had left early in a foul mood, and they expected to find him at the place where he'd left his musket – the burial mound. Yet all they found when they walked back that way was a strange looking British soldier with a bad leg sitting on a rock beside the burn.

They failed to notice the hastily concealed remains of a fire or the ripped off corporal stripes that lay scattered in the long grass beside the burial mound. Duncan was exhausted. He'd only just made it back to the burn before the first of the soldiers had appeared over the far ridge. He prayed that he'd muddied the jacket enough so that the patrol wouldn't recognise it for Dyker's. The men gathered about the stranger, curious as to where their corporal had gone.

"Hey, where's your patrol gone, mate?" questioned Private Jones. Duncan mustered up his courage and his best attempt at a more coarse Scottish tongue than his own.

"They went on ahead after treating ma leg... one of the blathering idiots shot me in the mist two days back. Haven't seen them since."

The Scots accent didn't surprise the English men; many highlanders had joined up on the side of the king, some even forming their clans into regiments. Most had had no say about who they fought with: their Laird said "go", and they went. Private DeWolfe stared long and hard at Duncan. Their eyes met, and at once the Scot knew that his disguise had been penetrated. He waited for the accusation.

"Oh," said DeWolfe eventually, his voice flat and unemotional. "You must be one of those Campbells."

"Aye I am that," replied Duncan eagerly, perhaps too eagerly; it might not only be DeWolfe who was suspicious. He was beginning to lose his temper. Why wouldn't this Sassenach just get the whole sorry business over and done with? He could out him and have a kill. Either he should challenge Duncan, or just leave him to eat his trout in peace.

DeWolfe stared at him for so long that the other soldiers began to lose interest, muttering among themselves about finding Dyker and tending to their ailments. A couple opened their tobacco pouches, and settled themselves down for a quiet draw on their stubby clay pipes. Someone would have to break the stand off, it might as well be Duncan.

"Ye wouldna have any vittals about ye? I lost mine when I was wounded." The unrefined accent of a mere crofter came hard to him, but he was learning fast. He thought back to the men, rowdy and blunt in his fields during harvest or rounding up sheep... his leg was throbbing... he'd heard that British soldiers were well cared for; might as well use them for everything that they had.

Jones scrabbled around in his untidy pack, at length producing a hunk of salted beef.

"We're looking for our corporal actually," he said, offering the meat to Duncan. "But we don't mind if we can't find him if you know what I mean." The British soldiers fell about laughing; DeWolfe stared hard at Duncan's eyes. The Scot grinned, but he did not really understand the joke. To try and cover up his confusion he looked at the salt beef and licked his lips, something that no self-respecting red coat would *ever* have done with the dire regulation army food.

Duncan opened wide his mouth and bit into the meat...and bit... and bit. Surely this piece of unmentionable shoe leather should be covering the hole in his – Dyker's – boot. A Laird of Duncan's standing couldn't eat foul stuff such as this, whatever the circumstances were. He moved the morsel around his teeth, and tried not to grimace. The laughter had died and they were all staring at him curiously; he had to be careful. Involuntarily wincing he ripped a lump of the beef into his mouth with a necessary force that made his teeth ache. He thought of the tender trout and choked.

*   *   *

Dyker opened his eyes at the sound of muffled voices. Had he been ill? His stomach was certainly very sore... but his jaw was pure agony! Then he remembered. The voices were indistinct – probably a whole tribe of wild Scotsmen. Damn them to hell and beyond! He may have been a coward, but he knew that he couldn't just lay there... they might want to eat him for want of better game. He exhaled slowly, composing himself.

"I've gotta git help..." he murmured between crusted lips that he dared not part due to the stinging tenderness.

He reached to pull a knife from his boot that he kept hidden for emergencies such as this, and found to his horror, that he was entirely naked! A nearby pile of what looked like old rags was all he had to cover his modesty. He was about to curse his vile luck, when a burst of laughter cut him short. The cries he could hear were *English*. If that was his patrol out there, then they would surely castrate the vile Scots filth who had done this to him; surely even that useless bunch of pansy slackers could shoot straight!

Climbing unsteadily, to his feet, and tying a long piece of the rough cloth around his waist, Dyker gingerly staggered towards the voices. Attempting to remain silent, he hissed through his teeth when he trod on a stone, his bare feet slipping on the wet sod. Having not looked at his 'attire' closely he had missed the distinct tartan patterning, covered in mud and dried bog water. So he proceeded, waiting until the talking had died down. He crouched, tensing like a coiled spring amidst the ferns, then launched himself into the daylight a strangled yell emanating from his swollen closed mouth as he ran through the highland heather like a man possessed.

The cry silenced everyone save Duncan, who swore under his breath at the interruption. Jones looked up and saw the wild shouting figure bearing down on him across the hillside. With an unfailing instinct he raised his loaded musket to his shoulder. Dyker, blundering downhill and unable to speak, waved his arms and yelled even more. His face was disfigured, but surely they could tell it was him -

"No, Jones! Stop lad!" several of his companions cried when they recognised their own corporal, but a sharp report, and a puff of blue smoke told them that it was too late. At that range even an English musket couldn't miss. The ball tore into his brain by his left temple. Dyker was stunned for a split second, a look of wonderment in his eyes until he crumpled forward into the heather as heavy as a hay bale.

Jones stood stock-still, his musket still raised.

Smoke drifted into his eyes, but he stared unblinking at the hated body in the heather.

Duncan tensed visibly and his grip tightened on his empty weapon as he waited for someone to question why Dyker was dressed in the garb of the enemy. The sweat stood out upon his brow, and he eyed the long sharp bayonets with apprehension. 'Christ Jesus,' he thought. 'Someone get it over with; I tried my hand and it failed. You win some, you lose some aye, and by God's will I've lost this time.'

He almost moved to speak, to admit his crime, when DeWolfe started to chuckle. Somebody else joined in and soon everyone was in hysterics, save for Duncan, and a white faced, shaking Jones.

"W – what have I done?" Jones said at length, a catch in his voice.

"Don't be so penitent," replied DeWolfe. "You hated him more than we did, that's all. No one could blame you for what happened. His disguise was better than any spy I've seen so far." Duncan caught the emphasis, and tried to work out what DeWolfe was planning. Either way he would have to go along with it.

"Looks like you're in charge now then, don't it mates?" Someone said, in a tone that suggested DeWolfe might have planned the whole thing. All eyes were on him and he lapped up the attention.

"But 'ow are we going to get back through that marsh?" a man asked nervously. "Dyker 'ad the map an' 'e could've stashed it anywhere." They could see base camp lying at the foot of the mountain, tantalisingly, close, but between it and them was the vast patch of bog that had nearly proved their undoing on the way up.

"I'm sure this chap can show us," mused DeWolfe, shrewdly. "He looks like a born leader. Used to be a corporal once, you can see where his stripes were. So lead on Macduff." The men looked to Duncan.

"*MacBain,*" muttered Duncan. "And I can show you the way, but I'm nae a corporal. Never have been."

"Very well," smiled DeWolfe, "You are now; and that means no running away. We know how to deal with corporals as you've witnessed." They moved off down the mountain, DeWolfe supporting Duncan, who felt like a mouse crouched beneath a cat's paw. Jones looked hard at the Scotsman.

"What the hell is going on?" he whispered.

Had he heard the words that DeWolfe hissed into the Laird's ear, he would have been even more confused. "Bluff..." Duncan said sourly, he felt the word eat into his brain. "And of course, the double bluff." Somehow, he felt base camp did not hold the same pleasures in store for him as for the rest of the eagerly returning men.

BRANDER

Brander tensed, and lifted his head in the manner of a dog casting for the scent of a fox. He sniffed the wind, a slight bitter odour set his nostrils tingling. Remaining as still as a rock he shifted his grip slightly on the crude but vicious spear. The balance had to be right or it would throw inaccurately. He wanted to kill.

A determined smile crept onto his face as he crouched in the peat hole, waiting for the strange smelling creature to show itself. Looking at this young man, he seemed no different from all the youths that hunted and fought in the hills, but the silver torque of a chieftain rested uneasily on his shoulders. His sword slept in a scabbard of blue goatskin banded with bronze. Seventeen years old and all the responsibilities of an elder. Alas, there was no enjoyment of childhood when the raven of time claimed its victims at forty or less.

A chief. To fight for, uphold the honour of, and die for the people of the túath. They were his tenets, a strict code that all the tribes understood. Wars were fought seasonally to an unwritten constitution of honour that butchered freemen and peasants. It gave chiefs the glory that would fit them for their great journey into eternity. Brander hated it.

He had begged and pleaded with his parents to send him away to the Holy Isle to study with the Druithin. Unfortunately the death of his father in a skirmish, a well respected chieftain, had thrust all the responsibility onto his eldest son. Of course he had tried to live up to his father's legacy, but everyone knew his heart wasn't in it. He was seldom even picked to go cattle raiding. It was not an action of charity towards him –

cattle were your wealth – it was because he was seen as a liability in the heat of battle.

Brander had never experienced real, gnawing, fear before. Tales of the strange-talking people, creatures from the south, had sent a wave of apprehension breaking over the heads of all but the most boastful chiefs. It left a tight feeling in their souls that nothing could dispel. No well-meaning sacrifice to the Gods could take away the pure facts, witnessed by their own incredulous eyes.

At first it had been peasants and a few freemen from other, more southerly, tribes. Then chiefs began to straggle in, many starving and wounded. There was a queer look about them, like that of a wolf at the end of a hunt. They appealed to Brander's túath for help. They asked their King for one last push against... against what? A heavily armoured, well trained, fighting machine that had relentlessly forced its way over all of southern Albion, and now up into the mid-lands.

Then the snows came as they did every year, and the strange people didn't. The men of the north waited. They were surrounded by the hills and mountains, covered with their annual mantle of snow and ice. In their waiting they grew complacent. Yet, with the green of spring came more refugees, tribal differences forgotten in the new race war. Something would have to be done. Food stocks would not last under the strain of this new onslaught of misery. Feelings were split between defending the land where they were, or launching a counter attack on their mutual foe to the south.

In a stirring speech at tribal council, Brander's lord berated all the chiefs for running around like confused ants. Where was their fighting spirit? Where was the cool calculation that had enabled them to amass such a high honour price of cattle? This situation could, and *should*, be treated like any other war. First send scouting patrols to find and count the foreigners' heads – maybe bring a few of those back with them. What kind of weak enemy couldn't brave the winter weather? Alien soldiers with constitutions like old women. Why, even someone like Brander could fight them!

There was general laughter, and Brander stood up sheepishly. Trying not to show his reluctance he dropped his sword at the lord's feet. The elder man smiled and patted him on the shoulder. Amidst general cheers many of the younger chiefs piled their weapons with his. This was going to be good sport. If Brander had actually volunteered for the fight it would only amount to a playful hunt. They had nothing to fear.

Outside the hut, the chiefs of the south lands shook their heads in pity, and prepared to move on, still further north into the wilds and away from their aggressors. They were too dispirited to rally and join with the túath. They had already witnessed so much destruction.

*   *   *

A soft movement in the long grasses. Rising on down-silenced wings was a good omen; a startled owl. Something had disturbed the druid-bird from its daytime slumber. Brander spun round, fresh sweat trickling down his furrowed brow. Nothing. Where were the weak foreigners now? Where were the weak old women who only fought in great shielded formations? No one had said that they had recruited soldiers from their Etruscan mountains, skilled in the art of hill fighting...

The young warrior chieftain crouched on the sun-drenched slope without even a boulder to shelter him. He thought back to that same morning... a hare chase. Frightened animals bounding across the grassy peat pursued by shouting young men, their voices echoing off the valley sides, giving their position away to everyone for at least five miles around.

He remembered stumbling across two bodies close together in the heather. One, a scrawny looking chief, had been pierced through the chest with a peculiar short sword. The other a darker skinned man, with some curious sort of body armour. He lay hunched up with the familiar Celtic blade buried firmly between his ribs. Brander had pushed the corpse onto its back with his foot, and the thin-lipped mouth sagged open, revealing two rows of dazzling white teeth. Hurriedly the Celt made the wolf sign to ward off this strange smelling demon-creature.

The slain man had suddenly opened his eyes and muttered something in a gibberish tongue! Terrified, Brander had slit the man's throat. His first kill, and no one to see the shame of it. His friends had disappeared over the brow of the hill, yelling at the hares and rabbits, while he had murdered an unarmed and wounded man. He had fled in humiliation, hiding his face.

Now there was a high pitched click of stone upon stone. The inexperienced chief glanced from the bright horizon to his sword which was lying on the black peat a few yards away. Could the approaching man see him? If he made a grab for the sword and tried to roll to the cover of a nearby patch of tall bog grass, would that foreign spear flash like lightening while he was in mid flight? Again a pebble chinked, he pivoted and hurled his own spear off to the right.

A quiet laugh told him that he'd fallen for the most basic trick, a child's game. Deception. Now what? He crouched down in the mud, weaponless, a sickly emptiness invading his young stomach. Why had he killed the wounded stranger when he could have taken him prisoner; but prisoner to what? Ritual slaughter? A revenge killing? He'd avenged his dead fellow tribesman by killing the foreigner laying half-dead in the bog, but the

47

shame... shame had to be washed out in the traditional manner. Brander desperately wanted a clean mind, free of guilt. It bothered him that to the guilt of not being an accomplished fighter, the humiliation of murdering a helpless man outside of battle had also been added... His mind took him back to the morning, it seemed so long ago tat he was forced to make another choice...

He had smelled a second soldier creeping up behind him as he crouched over the fallen chief and his first kill. A mixture of pungent, unfamiliar, spices and sweaty trepidation, much like the dead man at his feet. Brander had flashed around, his sword held at arm's length. The assailant's head had rolled clumsily through the tall yellow grasses, while Brander rejoiced in the new kill with a grin. He was finally blooded, a true warrior. Cleansed. His speed and skill would be spoken of for moons to come!

Although... He hadn't thought about how many soldiers there might be in the patrol. Soldiers wanting to find their two missing members. Their clansmen. The nearing sound of outlandish Latin voices had sent Brander running blindly away into the spongy peat hole. Fearing the worst, trying to avoid the treacherous wet ground, he'd tripped and dropped his sword. Oh praise him! A warrior who couldn't even fight sensibly. He was done for.

Now, he had been crouching for so long that his knees felt as if they would be locked in that position forever more. Any minute now the dark stranger who tricked him would throw his spear. Concentration was vital at this point. What would his wife do in this situation? How would she think her way out of it, she the meticulous swordswoman... He knew what the people thought of him and Enid... She would always surface victorious in any family squabble, or any inter-tribal duel. Her arms and legs – unlike his – bore the livid white scars as a testimony to her honour price.

Brander, the 'girl' chieftain. Not fit to lead a calf to water. Well, if only he could concentrate, he would show them. Two men dead, and possibly another if he could only gauge the offending spear throw and reach his sword all in the same movement. If only his mother had let him go to the Holy Island... no boy, pay attention. Now, here, this time should occupy all your senses, or there will be no future... Think. It is a life and death situation. Yet time seemed to have stood still. He felt 'outside' of reality...

"We'll be fixed like this, you and I, for many moons until the snows cover our bodies that have turned to stone..." he mused bleakly under his breath.

"*Brander!*"

The cry came wafting up from further down the hill. It was one of his men. A rescue! Someone must have found the slain bodies at the other end of the mire. Relief flooded through his aching body, relaxing, he turned on his hands and knees to face his village. He leapt to his feet, staring out over the beautiful green valleys and hills of his homeland, straining his eyes for a glimpse of his friend. It truly was a beautiful Isle. The warm mountain breeze instantly dried the beads of sweat from his forehead, gently flicking his long hair around his face.

High above him a golden eagle soared on powerful brown wings, Brander wished that he could be all-seeing like the great majestic bird. The eagle was always victorious. Blinded by the sun, he shaded his eyes with his hand and waited for the other chief to cross the near horizon. Perhaps it was the group back from chasing the hare. Together they could put the military patrol to flight – no bother at all...

*   *   *

A long, small headed, spear flashed leisurely in the sun. It found its target in the soft back of the Celtic chief, who was flung forward, carried by the swift weapon's momentum. Brander bit up a sour mouthful of the coarse black peat, dying instantly as the weapon pierced his heart.

The Roman auxiliary relaxed and sauntered over to the limp, young body, oblivious to the small fair-haired warrior who had crept up behind him with a long sword raised above her head in silent fury.

The eagle completed another smooth circle or the bogland and then flew off with a lonely screech. Hares were his prey. They never fought back.

MR DUBOIS

The October breeze was whipped up into a tumultuous gale during the night. By the time dawn revealed herself as a grey expanse of lowering cloud, the gusts of rain-spattered wind were singing their mournful autumn song in the branches of the ancient beech tree of the Duel Swords tavern. A title to evoke visions of hasty words and clashing blades, it was, in fact, taken from the two of swords, an ancient playing card that had decided the fate of the building as part of a bet. The most violent act it had witnessed was a sea cook who was bodily thrown out one night, not long after his money had gone the same way.

Stinging bullets of rain lashed Jem Timmons' face as he hurried about his daily business of feeding the family livestock. He had also been adjusting the ill-fitting wooden shutters on the stable windows, where the wind had shaken them free. He lingered a while at the pig sty, sharing dreams of riches and fame with his old friend.

Sarah was a placid Tamworth, who was in the latter stages of pregnancy. As the twelve year old boy watched the old hog wallow contentedly in the mud, the driving rain went unnoticed. Without a brother or sister to entertain him the pig had become his adopted sibling. She was a willing listener and never once complained, even when they ran out of food and she was forced to eat cabbage leaves for nine days straight. He patted her head and ruffled her ears back and forth. He was hoping to keep at least one of the litter, slowly building a small holding his father would have been proud of...

A distant shout brought the tousled young man out of his daily reverie, his blue eyes flashed, as the cold wind caught him by surprise. He put the empty swill bucket down, and wiped his hands on the bottom of a well worn, and likewise well soiled, waistcoat.

"Hail! You there! Boy!" came the cry again, "Can you assist me?" The caller stood about a quarter of a mile away up on the deserted cliff road – deserted, that is, except for the heavily muffled man and his untidy pile of baggage.

"Coming!" Jem yelled, the wind carrying his young voice easily to the stranger. "Custom at last..." he muttered to himself, and sprinted across the grassy cliff top towards the beckoning figure.

The wind pushed at him insistently from behind in forceful gusts, several times he had the sensation of almost being airborne. Suddenly, he stopped dead in his tracks, almost stumbling as the gale tried to carry him onward. The 'baggage' had moved. A stick like arm feebly grasped at the air, and then fell again. What could now be discerned as a sodden bundle of dark rags was actually a man.

"Quickly lad!" came the cry, "My friend is injured."

Jem flew on, almost colliding with the stranger, who grabbed his shoulders in a tight grip that spoke of both relief and desperation.

"Thank goodness you've come! I've been walking an hour or more into this wretched wind with my companion. We couldn't go on. I nearly fainted with relief when I saw the light from the inn." Jem stepped back, and looked the man up and down. Even *his* fairly innocent mind told him there was something odd going on.

He wanted to size up the situation before taking these two men back to the Duel Swords. Sick or otherwise, confidence tricksters were not unknown in these parts – men out on the scavenging lay – and he had no wish to be robbed or press-ganged into service for the King. The Navy, he had heard, would try anything, and he was not eager to wake up and find himself a powder monkey on one of his Majesty's ships of the line in

Portsmouth harbour... or worse, consigned to hard labour in the clink for aiding a criminal.

He looked down at the injured man, and noted the ugly hole torn by a musket ball in his left hip. Dark blood had stained the dirty cream of his breeches.

"You're smugglers?" he asked with such frankness that the upright man was somewhat taken aback – or so it seemed from what movement Jem could discern beneath the folds of his riding cloak.

"We are *loyal servants* of his Majesty, King George, and..."

"Are you *smugglers*?" pressed Jem.

"Well," the accent was refined and cautious after the initial panic. "At least we're not of the wrecking persuasion, you can be sure of that."

Jem spat into the grass, a habit his mother abhorred. She would have boxed his ears had she been present. He hated the wreckers, the scum who would deliberately lure a ship onto rocks and then strip her like maggots on a dead rabbit. It was almost certain that was how Jem's father had met his end. He had been a survivor from such a terrible wreck, well, a survivor until the cudgel on the beach had crushed the life from his brain...

Educated people, Jem thought enviously. An accent he couldn't quite place, but very high class for a smuggler. The stranger had more the appearance of a government spy. Better to be careful...

"It's alright, sir, I won't talk, I know better," was the only information that the boy gave. He had a natural distrust of people who tried to hide their background, and he had heard about a suspicious new Riding Officer being stationed about ten miles along the coast.

However, he had been brought up to be polite to his elders, though the stranger would have to part with more information if he wanted shelter. He proved to be forthcoming.

"The Revenue delighted in using us for target practice last night. We were lucky to escape with our lives. They had the militia waiting for us. Some poor fellows would only have left that beach face down on a shutter…" Suddenly the man now seemed to have the tongue of a scatter brained girl! Or was he trying to convince the boy that he was someone other than his true self?

Jem was beginning to wish that'd he'd ignored the initial cry for help, or had gone to fetch his mother. Being the man of the family had its disadvantages, particularly when you were only shoulder-high. The weather chose that moment to become much worse. A flash of lightning was immediately followed by a clap of thunder so loud that the men were temporarily deafened. It heralded a solid downpour of rain that dropped like a heavy curtain. Everything was blotted from view, and all three of them were soaked to the skin before they could even decide on a plan of action.

"We must take your friend inside, out of the storm!" Jem found himself shouting. There was no point in trying to keep the wounded man dry. Were those deep ragged rends in the stranger's cloak sabre cuts? The tall man supported his friend on one side, while Jem hoisted his shoulders under his limp, dragging arm. He shivered – not from the wet. The whole body was icy cold against him, even more so than the rain. The boy unaccountably felt the hairs on the back of his neck rise. He felt odd in his stomach. Although he was not breaking the law of humanity, it was the first time he had broken the law of the land… and what would his mother say to their two new bedraggled guests?

The injured party began to moan, and feebly struggle as he was dragged through the door of the Duel Swords. Any cleansing action that the rain may have had on Jem's waistcoat was offset by the blood that had soaked into it, making him wonder if the man wasn't maybe beyond saving already. Certainly he – Jem –

would be beyond saving if the blood would not wash out. Still, trade was poor out on the cliffs, and perhaps the educated gentleman had a purse full of gold sovereigns. Jem had never heard tell of an impoverished 'trader', and if he *was* a Revenue agent, the boy thought it would not be a bad idea to relieve him of every penny that he could. Besides, he grudgingly admitted to himself for the umpteenth time, they couldn't leave anyone to die on their doorstep.

"Oh my goodness; saints save us from ourselves!" cried out Mrs Timmons, in horror. Her hands flew to her face, and she took a pace backwards. "What *have* you been *doing*?" The stranger said not a word, but helped Jem to drape the wounded man over an empty table. After struggling out of his sodden cloak, he and the boy proceeded to lay his companion flat on his back, and started to remove his clothing.

"Oh, Jem, Jem… get away to Dr Parker, and tell him we have a *very* sick man here," Jem's mother drew closer, but appeared not to see the blood for all her worried glances.

"Mother, hold your haste!" If he was the man of the family, he would act like he'd seen other men behave. The stranger at his side gave him a peculiar confidence, something that he'd never felt when dealing with his mother before, and certainly not when he knew he was in the wrong from the off.

"I would prefer not to have the doctor here, ma'am," said the man, without looking up from his work. "There would be the need for awkward questions that the sawbones might feel were best answered… in front of a law officer. No, no we must tend my friend as best we can. Mrs Timmons – don't worry, Jem has told me your name – I would be obliged for some hot water, and then perhaps use of a bed…"

"I'll help you get him upstairs," said Jem without daring to look at his mother.

Twenty minutes later the wounded man lay bandaged, still comatose, in one of the empty guest rooms. Jem had been despatched to his own bedroom to change out of his wet, stained clothes. Mrs Timmons was tidying up the sopping mess downstairs as best she could, while the tall stranger had returned to the bar to make sure that there were as few signs of their muddy arrival left to view as possible.

The boy went to the top of the staircase, where he paused. From here he could look over the dark oak banisters – polished by wear, as much as by his mother – and observe the man without being obtrusive. Taking a closer look at his clothing all hope of gold sovereigns evaporated. If he was in the 'trade' then he was either just starting out, or not very good at it! Maybe he was in disguise? The clothes had obviously once been very fine, but now they looked as though nothing was holding them together. Yet, they did not appear patched or darned.

All the elegant finery of London's last 'season' hung from the lean body as he knelt down and mopped at the footprints on the floor with a dirty rag... and the garments looked as though they had been wet for a lot longer than just the last hour or so. Great patches of powdery mildew stained the blue satin. Possibly a distressed 'Gentleman of Fortune'... very obviously in need of a decent meal. Jem noted the sallow complexion, protruding cheek bones, and the sunken yellowed eyes.

Just then those eyes looked up, and the boy hurriedly clattered downstairs, wondering if these two 'clients' would be able to pay anything at all. Sick or not, his mother would have a few choice words to say on the matter if their purses were empty. He offered the stranger a mug of ale, but the man said that he would prefer port, given the soaking he'd just had, and that – by the way – he went by the name of Gilbert Dubois, from out by Bridport.

"Is that where the run was last night?" questioned Jem excitedly, before he could stop himself.

"Good heavens, no," once again here was the almost girlish desire to give away more details. "We were down by Seatown, just after midnight. Nigh on five of us were killed. I think we would have lost all our cargo... you tend not to look back when a musket – or a noose – is hard on your heels." Seatown? That was where the Walters gang operated from. The brothers were regulars; about the only regular drinkers at the inn these days. There certainly hadn't been any run scheduled last night, for they'd been nursing their beers until nearly eleven and would have been in no condition to 'run' anywhere. Though... there had been rumours of a split in the organisation...

Perhaps someone else had tried a landing? He looked sideways at Mr Dubois, but that oddly clad gentleman was deeply involved in the port and the warmth of the fire. The man was obviously still very cold, for despite the heat of the flames no steam was rising from his clothes.

"I would offer you a change of clothing, sir," said Mrs Timmons, entering the room. "But my husband's have all been long used up, and t'is obvious the boy's won't fit."

"It is of little consequence, ma'am. I have been wetted before, and will no doubt be so again. You get used to the deplorable condition."

Jem still didn't trust the man. He found that his mind would not focus properly on current events. Obviously he wouldn't have heard any shooting last night, because the wind was blowing from the inn towards the bay, so the story was feasible. Another thought struck him, like the blow from a fist.

"Mr Dubois," he began, and startled himself with the loudness of his voice in the empty parlour. "Mr Dubois, were you chased – followed – by any soldiers...?" Two pale watery eyes stared at him over the top of the glass.

"To begin with, certainly. But when the storm grew bad, I think they retreated..." He shook his head, "No, I can't say for certain. It was very dark and windy back there."

Jem turned away from the man, and screwed his face up into a concentrated frown. A Revenue officer leading the soldiers to suspected smugglers – first find out your information, then make the arrest... then what about the other man upstairs? He was certainly in a bad way, and a law man would not help a smuggler to escape. But had the ball in his leg come from a soldier's musket, or a smuggler's pistol? He had to act fast, before his mother started panicking.

"Sir, you will realise that if you were followed here, it would go badly for my innocent mother and myself; especially if they find you still within..." He scrutinised the man's face for a sign of betrayed emotion, but there was not a flicker of movement.

"So then, you must hide us away until we can arrange for a safe passage away from here. We do not wish to bring you misfortune." His mother was growing concerned.

"Jem, we can't move that poor man again..."

"Mother, we have no choice!" Mr Dubois interrupted.

"I think the lad has made a very sensible point, ma'am, but alas, to try and move my companion very far will mean almost certain death to him."

"Please excuse us Sir," Jem tried to stop his voice from shaking, "Mother, will you come into the kitchen for a moment?" She followed him, as if in some kind of dream. It was the day of John's demise all over again – strangers in the parlour, blood, fear... "Listen, Ma, I think that those two may be working for the Revenue. Mr Dubois is far too well dressed to be in the trade. If the Walters come back in here tonight they may find themselves trapped."

"Oh, Jem, what have you done, bringing 'em here? I wish you'd left them out on the cliff. That one upstairs he won't get dry however much I towel him. I don't want any trouble."

Although he fully appreciated the danger of the situation, Jem was beginning to enjoy himself. The events of the morning had sent so much adrenalin coursing through his veins that he felt ready to take on half the Revenue single handed. His mind seemed full of ingenious schemes to fit any eventuality.

"If we were to put them in the old keg cellar under the cliff, they'd be dry, but they'd also be out of the way. We'd know where they are, but they wouldn't be able to hear anything that was going on in the bar." Mrs Timmons chewed her lip anxiously.

"Oh, well, I suppose we could, but what if the soldiers come…"

"Simple; if they *are* who they say they *are* they will be hidden in the old cellar, and the soldiers needn't find them. If they're spies they'll be out of the way and won't hear anything they shouldn't. Robin Walters will know what to do with them for sure."

"Well, I just hope you know what you're doing. What'd your father would think? I've got no idea, God rest his poor soul." So saying, she bustled back into the bar's parlour. Dubois had not stirred from his place in front of the fire.

"Mr Dewbar, I will make no bones about the fact that I am not happy with what's going on here. I have always kept a respectable house, and intend to carry on doing so. But I don't like to see men unfairly put upon, and your friend is in no condition to state his case. We can put you somewhere safe, until he is well enough to leave. It is the old cellar of the inn, once used by 'traders', but long standing empty." Mr Dubois' eyes raised from the fire. "You are welcome to the room until your friend is mended. But once he can walk I want you gone."

"Your generosity is far greater than I deserve, ma'am." The gentleman said. "We shall be no trouble once we are stowed away. As God is my witness."

"Jem, show Mr Dewbar where it is." He walked up to one of the dark wooden panels beside the staircase, and kicked the bottom skirting, hard. There was a sharp click, as a hidden catch was released, and the panel creaked open towards the boy. A thin flight of steps led down into darkness that a candle revealed as a square chamber carved in the rocky cliff below the inn.

Jem carefully descended, walked across the room and unhitched a shutter on one of the walls. Grey daylight flooded in, and fresh draughts moved one or two cobwebs that hung from the limestone ceiling. With a great deal of difficulty they edged the wounded man down the narrow stairs, one at a time. Mrs Timmons piled bedding on the dry, dusty floor for him to lie on. Jem then brought down a candle, the rest of the bottle of port, a loaf of bread, and some cheese.

"Poor fare, I'm afraid sirs," said his mother. "But it will see you through the rest of the day. Tonight we will bring you something warmer."

"And I'll let you know if anyone comes asking for you," added Jem. "If the draught from the window is too much you'll have to put up the shutter and use the candle."

"I am sure we will get by most admirably," Mr Dubois smiled, and inclined his head slightly. With that the boy and his mother climbed back up the smooth stone steps, and closed the secret panel. Mrs Timmons then collapsed into a chair, motioning to Jem to pour her a large brandy – for 'her nerves'.

"What are we doing son?" she asked, "What on God's green earth are we *doing*?"

*　　　*　　　*

60

Just after lunch time (one that saw no customer braving the inclement weather, for which Mrs Timmons was secretly glad), the sow went into a prolonged, and rather difficult labour. It was thus not until about seven of the clock, when the sound of an evening customer hammering on the door took her back to the inn. Jem realised the gusts of wind had dropped, and was thankful that none of the tiles had come loose on the outbuildings or the Duel Swords.

Wearily leaving Sarah suckling her new litter in the shelter of the barn, he went outside and looked up at the night sky. A few clouds scudded across the stars, silver edged by moonlight against the storm-washed blackness. He glanced down at the dead piglet in his hand, and threw it with all his strength out into the darkness beyond the cliff edge "...for the fishes."

Later that evening Jem sat hunched over the large table in the parlour of the bar. His eyelids were drooping, and his head kept sagging until his chin knocked against his pewter mug. This woke him up slightly, but eventually his mother came over, drawn by the laughter and comments of the Walters brothers. They had been discussing a 'run' that was to take place the following week and with their preparations over they were finding the boy's attempts at staying alert most amusing.

"Jem, get up those stairs to your bed," said his mother, brusquely, but not unkindly. "You're no use to me here." The boy was too punch drunk to reply, but merely hauled himself unsteadily to his feet and made his way, zombie like, to the stairs.

"Eh, Mrs, you should train him to hold his drink better," called Robin Walters, "'E won't make a landlord if'n he falls asleep afore ten o'clock!"

"Yes, well, if those as is still drinking would care to finish up; the pair of us have had a terrible day of it, and could do with an early night. We'll be right as rain tomorrow."

Robin Walters shrugged and winked.

"Huh, seems as though we had enough rain today already, don't need more tomorrow!" Mugs and tankards were hurriedly drained, the men moved out into the still night. Mrs Timmons followed close by to lock the door behind them.

"Pity about the moon," one of them said, looking at the empty sky. "T'will still be at the quarter on the night."

"Still means we can see them before they see us," said another. "All that pretty harness a-sparkling and…"

"Hold your chatter," commanded Robin curtly, "Goodnight, Mrs."

"Goodnight Sir." Mrs Timmons smiled tiredly, plainly, as if she didn't understand what was going on. She had known Robin Walters for over five years and had quite a soft spot for him. The feelings were probably reciprocated, judging by the fact that he was careful – albeit unsuccessfully – to shield her from his nocturnal activities.

*   *   *

It was late in the morning when fingers of sunlight worked their way through the cracks in the shutters to touch the closed eyes of Jem Timmons. He awoke, and lay for a moment, listening to his mother moving around in the bar downstairs. His stomach felt empty, and he wondered if she had milked the cow; a mug of fresh milk and a couple of warm biscuits would set him up nicely to face the day ahead.

Then realisation dawned on him, and he leapt from his bed with a cry, running downstairs two at a time, his nightshirt billowing around his skinny legs.

"Ma, Ma, we left those men in the cellar without food! They'll be half frozen…" But his mother was already at the panel by the stairs. The door swung open, and as Jem joined her, they could tell by the darkness at the bottom of the steps that the shutter of the cellar was up. There was no candle lit either! Jem took a taper and lit one of the from the bar to use as a crude torch.

Carefully shielding the flame from draughts he cautiously proceeded down the steps, the stone chilling his bare feet. He went as fast as he dared to the shutter, and took it down, instantly snuffing the candle with the invigorating sea breeze that came in from the side of the cliff. Although he'd sensed it as he crossed the room, the sunlight confirmed his confusion: the cellar was deserted.

There was no trace of it having ever been used since it was shut up all those years ago. Cobwebs still wafted in the air currents, long and white, like spectres hanging down unbroken by human activity. The film of dust on the floor lay undisturbed, save for the prints of Jem's bare feet where he had run across from the stairs.

Of the candle sconce that he had left with the two men, there was no sign, until he suddenly realised that the one he'd picked up from the table was the same one he'd used yesterday. But how had it been back in the parlour? The door only opened one way... When he put the question to his mother, she seemed of the opinion that the men had taken the food they'd been given, and had sneaked out through the bar during the evening, before she'd locked up.

"And good riddance, I say. We can only hope they didn't hear anything they shouldn't have when the Walters were here." She pulled her shawl tighter around her shoulders.

"But, Ma, you can't get out of the cellar from this side. The hinges don't work like that." She sniffed, a little disgruntled that Jem could be correct.

"Huh, that wood is pretty old. I expect it gives easy enough to the push of a boot or two."

"Well, let's try it. You go..."

"I'm not going anywhere, my lad! T'is after ten, and you're standing down here in your shift, fit to catch your death of cold or chill. Up and dressed with you. I've done with the cow, and Sarah's quite comfortable too."

"Oh, but…"

"Don't you 'but' me Jem Timmons. Go and get dressed, get a spot of breakfast, then you can clean this cellar out good and proper. Having opened it again, we might as well make some proper use of it." She bustled him up the stairs, and didn't let him out of her sight until he'd washed, dressed, and breakfasted.

"Now, you take a broom to that cellar, while I see what I can do with those ruined things of yours from yesterday. Covered in mould and mud, they are!"

No, he thought, that's not right. Mud and blood, perhaps, but mould? They hadn't been wet for long enough. Oh, well, if his mother thought that she could get the dirt out easily it was no concern of his. Perhaps the blood had washed off in the rain. Rats; he wouldn't be able to show the heroic stains to his friends now. Still, just as well; other people might notice, and then start asking awkward questions... though he wasn't convinced that the pair could have just left like that... He was more inclined to think that the wounded man would not have lasted the night. Desperate times drove men to do desperate things, maybe they'd scaled the cliffs and made their exit that way. Well, good luck to 'em. And if they were Revenue… well, part of him hoped they'd fallen over the edge in the dark.

*　　　*　　　*

The night after the run found the parlour of the Duel Swords full to bursting. Not only were the men involved pleased with their haul, but the morning light had revealed a mystery which was the talk of the village. Now the story was being discussed, and 'improved' on the cliff top. As far as Jem could make out what had happened was as follows:

A group of smugglers, returning to their homes by a round about route, had noticed what looked like – in the half light of dawn – a rotting sack partly submerged in a patch of bog on the heath. When someone investigated further, to see if the large bag contained anything valuable, it was found to be the decomposing corpse of a man wrapped in a riding cloak! It had obviously been lying in the reeds for a number of months, and looked as though the local wildlife had taken an interest in it.

This discovery had left the men in a dilemma. By rights, they should have reported the body to the local magistrate, but questions were bound to be asked as to what they were doing out on the heath at six of an autumn morning before sunrise. Even if smuggling was not suggested, a few local landowners might wonder about poachers. After a heated discussion, the disgusting object was picked up with as much reverence as possible and carried to the churchyard, where it was left beneath one of the yew trees.

The discovery of this grisly gift put the local verger into a state of near hysteria, and the vicar had to calm him down with a dose of strong gin. The sexton (who had been quietly informed of where the corpse had come from), searched through what was left of the man's clothing for any form of identification.

Other than describing him as "probably a Frenchy", nothing could be gleaned from the body in its current state. There was no visible sign of foul play, due to the decomposition of the flesh. So, at present the corpse resided in a rough wooden coffin in the sexton's shed, while the Squire arranged an official inquest. An opinion had been gently circulated that the dead man had been stolen from a gibbet somewhere and dumped in the churchyard as a prank. The verger would not go near it, and the vicar thought the humour was tasteless, sacrilegious, and infantile. The best thing as far as he was concerned was to give the man a decent burial as soon as possible and put his soul to rest.

The gentlemen drinking at the Duel Swords knew better, of course. They had worked out that the corpse was likely to have been that of a fashionable man from London, who had come down to watch a run back in the summer for a bit of sport. This particular operation had been noted for its failure, and several people in the Walters gang had gone to meet their maker. One or two others had been detained at his Majesty's pleasure, but after a couple of weeks they had been freed due to lack of evidence. The stranger from London – and a companion – had presumably fled when the fun became too dangerous for their liking.

A simple headstone was raised above the grave, with the year of death and a short passage from scripture. The corpse became old news, and people had other things to think about as autumn moved on to Christmas... a festival which was celebrated in weather that was cold, damp, and dismal without the delight of winter snow painting the world white.

*   *   *

The first of the January gales had blown itself to a long awaited standstill, leaving behind the usual trail of damaged buildings and fallen trees. Jem was wandering around outside the Duel Swords, picking up broken slates, and trying to see whether there were any actual holes in the roof. A breeze still sighed dolefully in the branches of the old oak tree, and leaden clouds hung over the cliff road like a flock of dirty sheep.

Jem was just contemplating the broken splinters of the inn sign, as it swung awkwardly from a single hook, when he heard a voice.

"Hail! Can you assist me?" The words sent a shock of fear coursing through the boy's body, as recognition sparked in his brain. No, he said to himself, no; surely he was imagining it. But, as he focussed his eyes, he saw the vision that had haunted his nights' sleep for the past three months. The stranger was there, but this time alone. Again the man called out, and this time Jem was conscious of the fact that Mr Dubois was speaking into the wind, yet was still perfectly audible.

Time seemed to slow right down, and the lad stood rooted to the spot for what felt like a lifetime. When he eventually managed to force his legs to move out onto the road, he had the sensation of wading through heavy surf at low tide. His mind had dulled, and he went forward unquestioningly, like a sleepwalker. All the time Mr Dubois was beckoning, reeling Jem in on an invisible line. Before the boy actually reached him he started to move away, still beckoning. His garb was exactly the same as before, and Jem vaguely noted the same mould stains adorning his clothes, the sabre cuts were there in the heavy material of the cloak.

"My friend is trapped in a foul marsh over on some heathland yonder. Please help me. I'm sure you can…" He gave no indication that he'd ever met Jem before, he simply turned and moved away.

Although his knees felt that they were about to give way beneath him with fear, Jem followed. His footsteps fell in time with the dull thud of the blood pounding in his head, and the air felt thick in his ears, like he was listening to everything through several blankets. The two figures – man and boy – moved slowly on in some kind of grotesque dance. They saw no one, and it seemed as though they were the only two people left in the entire world.

At last they came upon the clifftop heath, though Jem could not remember which route they had taken. Sure enough, Mr Dubois had been correct. There was another mud-caked individual struggling up to his chest in the black, clutching, mire. Falling to his knees, the youth dipped his hands into the cold, wet, mud and hooked them under the man's armpits. Then he braced himself, and pulled.

He did not notice that Mr Dubois offered no assistance. There was a sudden movement on the part of the trapped man, and for a moment Jem thought he was going to be pulled into the bog head first, but he regained his balance, and dug his knees into the wet moss.

The man was incredibly light for his apparent size... after not too much effort on Jem's part, with a loud sucking noise the clinging swamp gave way. Jem toppled backwards, and the man flopped on top of him, moaning in agony. He was very thin; all Jem could feel was skin and bone through the sodden clothing. As he extricated himself, the boy almost choked on the rank breath coming from his open mouth. He smelled like the corpse of a rotting sheep that Jem had once stumbled across.

Getting himself up onto all fours, he was horrified, but not surprised, to recognise the injured man from the previous incident – still, it seemed, with the same wound in his leg. The boy felt as though he was acting out one of his own nightmares, but he found himself powerless to break out of the sequence. His brain became sluggish every time he tried to question his circumstances.

Mr Dubois uttered a hasty word of thanks, and drifted off in the general direction of the village, moving like someone who had been there before, but not confident of the exact route to take. Jem, too scared to approach the injured man (and too curious to let Mr Dubois out of his sight), followed the bizarre gentleman at a distance. In doing this he noticed a curious occurrence.

Whenever he drew within about thirty feet of the figure, his brain went into the soporific state of acceptance as it had done earlier on, but as long as he held back he could think and react normally. This in itself galvanised his growing curiosity, and he once more wondered if Mr Dubois was in the pay of the government. Was he shrouded by some potion or tonic that could affect people nearby? Was it witchcraft?

Mr Dubois increased his pace as he neared the village, and strode into the narrow high street, as if making for the courthouse. Jem nodded sagely to himself, yet when he looked up to concentrate on the figure, his quarry had gone... and with his passing the strange heaviness had lifted from the air. The boy found himself alone in the centre of the cobbled road, and saw that he was standing by the churchyard. He looked all around, the street was deserted. A farmer appeared at the far end, leading a horse. Jem approached him and asked if he'd seen anyone pass by.

"No, lad," came the reply. "T'is uncommon quiet here today. I've seen more folk at a fox's funeral."

The only thing for it was to go back to the heath to see if the injured man was there. Perhaps this was all just a ghastly dream – or perhaps the incident in October had been a dream...? After all, his mother did not seem to have been too upset by it. The answer must lie with the wounded man.

To shorten his journey, he left the road, and cut through the graveyard next to the church. In winter the sexton tended to let nature take its course, so most of the graves were slightly overgrown. Everything was covered by a mat of wet, brown, leaves. Inscriptions were difficult to read on stones sporting coats of green algae, leaving odd letters peering out like stonemasons' anagrams. All save for one headstone, set apart from the others on a clear piece of ground, where grass had still not established a firm hold over the hummock of spade-compressed soil.

Although he'd passed this place several times a week in the month since the fresh stone was erected, he found his eyes, and then his body, drawn inextricably towards the lonely grave. As he read the neat lettering, everything seemed to make a terrible kind of sense. The original inscription had been altered and it now read:

Here lie the mortal remains of
Gilbert Dubois, 1721 to 1754
killed before his appointed time by man and nature.
May he rest in peace.

A hand clamped down suddenly on Jem's shoulder, and he jerked sideways, crying out in alarm. His heart briefly stopped (he would later say) and then began pounding furiously against his ribs like a mallet. But when he turned round, it was only one of his village school friends. The boy was hopping from foot to foot with excitement, grinning all over his face.
"What d'you think, Jemmy? You're missing all the fun! They've found another corpse up at the heath. Reckon it's been in the bog since last summer, like the other...."
The lad trailed off, as he realised that his friend was looking decidedly ill. The colour had drained from Jem's face, and he staggered, clutching at the headstone for support. He took several deep breaths, while his companion surveyed him quizzically.
"Here, be you alright Jem? Looks like you see'd a ghost..."

ON THE RUN

October 1962, Yorkshire.

It was just the place he'd been looking for: near enough to the prison to ensure that it would have already been searched, and far enough away from any other habitation to be left alone. For close on two hours Larry had crouched beneath the hedge, staring at the little stone house for any signs of life. He was cold, soaked to the skin but – most importantly – free. Free of that forbidding structure out there on the moors; free to tell the tale his way, and hopefully get someone to listen this time. He could only hope...

A movement by the front door... it was that fat girl again, carrying a metal bucket of scraps over to what seemed like a pigsty. Certainly there were porcine sounds issuing forth. In two hours she'd been the only person he'd seen; feeding the rangy chickens that scuttled about with bedraggled feathers, trying to burn some damp rubbish (on which she gave up) and weeding the small front garden. She seemed oblivious to the drizzle. No sign of a man anywhere. Perfect.

A soft rustling noise came to his ears; a breeze snaked through the hedge. Soon it was raining in earnest. Huge drops of icy water began to fall from the leaves onto his head. A chill north wind had sprung up and he started to shiver. The large girl muttered something, put down her bucket, stumped into the house and slammed the front door.

It wasn't until the rain had increased to a steady downpour that he ventured into the fading light of the late autumn afternoon. Across the rectangle of flat lawn he could now see the house more easily. It was a solid, dependable cottage, built from the same dull stone as the

71

prison, but so much more inviting. Knowing that he was invisible to anyone but those in the house, he shambled across the sodden grass. His feet sloshed through the puddles that were becoming small grey lakes in a surrounding carpet of faded green moss which had over-taken the grass.

It was whilst standing in one of these pools that he paused for a moment. What if there were more people there? What if they turned him in? Perhaps he should avoid human beings altogether until he was further away... The frigid water pouring down his neck made him almost long for his dry prison bed – at least it was warm and you got two square meals a day – but he knew what he had to do. Without another thought he strode forward and banged on the flaking blue paint of the front door.

He was just about to knock again when there was the click of a latch, and he found himself looking through an inch wide gap into a single, shining, unblinking, eye.

"What d'you want?" The voice was a rich contralto, laced with the local accent.

"Please, I..." A screeching shout from inside the house interrupted him.

"*Who is it? What's ta want!*" Larry hesitated; perhaps he'd better run now. He'd made a mistake, there was someone else inside.

"Hold up Gran, I haven't asked him yet," came the sweet voice again.

The door opened slightly, and he could see two eyes shimmering brightly in the shadows. They seemed to be rather close set, and squinting. He shivered.

"Please ma'am, I'm lost, and it's pis... *pouring* down out here. Could I come in? Maybe I could use your phone..."

"Got no telephone." Good, he thought. The eyes were gone and he could make out the back of a head. "Young chap. Wants to get out of t'rain." Again the anonymous screech from within.

"*Put 'im in t'barn then lass!*"

"But, Gran, he's soaked through, and…"

Here the girl lowered her voice, and Larry felt as though he'd been forgotten. If he stayed out here much longer he'd be washed away in the deluge, catch his death of cold on the moor, or be picked up by the officers searching for him. Well, the least he could do was shelter in the hallway. Before he could move forward the door swung open, making him step back in surprise. He wiped the curtain of rain-soaked hair from his eyes with the back of his hand, and for the first time saw the large girl in the daylight up close. Never, he was sure, had he seen someone quite as ugly as this young woman.

She did not have the hideous disfigurement of some accident, but she was more hideous than simply the bland, puffy, features of an obese 'Plain Jane'. The poor girl, her face liberally smeared with farmyard grime, was really stomach-turning. He stood transfixed, as an expression of disgust crossed his face, to be quickly replaced with one of pity – but those bright eyes of hers had picked up every subtle change. He couldn't help but be initially shocked, he was only human after all. He wondered if this made him a dreadful person for judging her instantly, outwardly…

To begin with she was fat, no, obese. Probably a glandular deficiency that turned her into a shape reminiscent of a swollen beer barrel. He realised that this effect was partly created by three layers of rough winter clothing, none of it clean. The garments were obviously too small for her frame. A kind way to describe her face would be 'pig-like', but the skin seemed yellow and unhealthy in the dim daylight coming through the doorway. There were dark blueish bags under her eyes. He noted that her hair was a dirty mahogany, and unfortunately she was covered with it. The backs of her unwashed hands seemed to be carpeted with a thick down, making her resemble an ape. She was clearly suffering from some ailment.

"Come in if you're coming..." she mumbled, seemingly embarrassed by his pure disgust. "You'll catch your death."

At least her voice seemed normal, and he stepped thankfully from the cold rain into the close confinement of the dark hallway. Once the door was shut, it was pitch black in the house, and he found himself blind. However, what his eyes couldn't see, his nose could detect. A powerful female odour made his eyes water, and he fought back the urge to choke. It was as if an unwashed horde of hookers had been using the cottage as a brothel. Larry was suddenly feeling less than confident; more and more uneasy. He was the one who should be in charge of the situation, he was the dangerous run-away demanding refuge, not this ignorant farm girl that he could not even see.

What was she doing now; just standing in the dark... breathing heavily... Something brushed against his right thigh and a deep sigh came to his ears. She was touching herself inappropriately, hidden in the blackness. 'Oh no, please, not that,' he thought and desperately tried to find the door handle behind him to escape; but the girl was suddenly there and his hand touched her. He recoiled in horror as another excited sigh filled the hall, he was regretting this arrangement and in his confusion he stumbled into the girl. She manoeuvred herself between him and the only means of exit.

"Come on then," the deep, almost sensuous, contralto relieved the tension a little. "Come and see Granny."

The room that he was shown into was lit only slightly better than the hall. In fact there was no artificial lighting, just a dull grey glow as the murky twilight struggled in through filthy net curtains. After the mine-shaft of the hall, to Larry's eyes it was positively floodlit. Directly in front of him was a huge fireplace, cavernous and black. Stepping into the room he had the impression of a gigantic mouth waiting to swallow him up. The whole atmosphere of this cottage was stifling. Either that or he was getting a cold; he felt hot, even though no fire burned in the grate, and his clothes dripped cold water onto the rush matting that covered the floor instead of a carpet or rug.

"Come over here, lad. I canna see thee." He had never got used to that accent. All the warders had it, and it made the convicts from the south feel as though they were prisoners of war in a foreign land. Perhaps it was partly this that had spurred him on to escape, to flee this barren landscape of hills and low heather where it always seemed to be raining. He wished to return to the orchards and sun of Kent; that, and to get hold of the bastard who had got him framed in the first place. "Come over to t'window, lad, t'is too dark to see thee proper." The voice was no longer the screeching banshee of a few minutes earlier, it had dwindled to a menacing croak.

"It *is* getting a bit dark outside," ventured Larry, "Perhaps you should put the light on..."

"Southerner art 'ou, lad?" was the old woman's reply.

"Yes," came the answer warily, "what of it? And what about some light. I can hardly see you either -" he said with more vigour than he felt in his heart.

"Spirit too. Good. That'll keep *you* going for a while, lass." This last remark was addressed to the mound of a girl who giggled expectantly from a dark corner of the room.

Larry had been patient long enough. Slowly he began to back towards the internal door, his left hand groping behind him for the handle. He shot forward, almost into the fireplace, when his fingers were buried between two enormous warm thighs instead. The huge girl chuckled again, mocking him. Panting from the shock, his head reeling with worry, he heard the snap of a key turning in the lock. Shit, he'd really screwed up on this one. He didn't even have a criminal instinct for trouble. No wonder he'd been caught out before... What a damn fool...

"Cup o' tea on't table lad, and a jam butty," the old woman stated, as if this was an expected visit.

Hunger rapidly overcame fear and he fell on the food, tearing off great chunks of fresh bread and washing it down with draughts of strong sweet tea. He couldn't remember when he'd last eaten home cooked food, and the prison slop had been plain porridge or dry bread, then a stew of indescribably meat and vegetables every night for dinner. This spread was practically manna from Heaven. Once more he regretted not arming himself. He didn't even have a butter knife with which to threaten these two peculiar women. It seemed that they had carefully removed all the cutlery from the table before he came into the room. Still he *had* to take command of the situation.

He pushed the last morsel of sweet jammy bread into his mouth and swallowed hard.

"Right," he snapped, turning to face them. He hoped he sounded threatening and confident. "From now on you women'll listen to me." Silence, the silence of fear... But it should not have been his own fear. This was all wrong. "Now then, the police are looking for me and..."

"Aye, we heard t'siren." mused the old woman.

"Aye," came a voice from just behind his right ear, "It's always *very exciting* when the siren goes." Larry shuddered and tried to regain the last of his mettle.

"As long as you do as I tell you, you won't get hurt, see..."

The old woman's cackling laughter made the hairs on his neck strain to attention

"Eh, you're just like t'last, lad!" she squealed. He felt a nasty taste in his mouth and peered at the crone through the gloom. She was grinning, broken teeth showing between her thin lips.

"The – the last one, what do you mean?" he asked.

"We're that close to t'prison, we've always got boys like

76

you passin' by here seeking shelter." Suddenly realisation dawned and he relaxed slightly.

"Ah, you mean you're a *ferrying point*? A halfway house? You know people that can help move me on?"

Another burst of laughter, this time he joined in, albeit nervously.

"Aye, you *could* say that." The huge girl was at his side and brushed his hip with her fingertips. He tensed but slowly eased. This wasn't too bad, why *should* it matter what state the cottage was kept in, it seemed dry enough, and the smell seemed to have subsided now he was in the main room. Must have been a pile of dirty washing in the hallway. This place would certainly do until the rain passed, or eased off a little.

So this was their method. They helped people away from the prison in turn for 'favours' for the ugly granddaughter. Maybe they were trying to get her pregnant, a child in the house could mean they got assistance from the council for things, benefits, grants... He let his mind wander. One night with a beast was preferable to going back to that pit of a prison. His cell mate was unhinged, deranged, and he had spent every night with one eye open for fear he would end up another prison statistic; dead before the age of thirty. He would have to grin and bear it. As long as he wasn't expected to pay for his time with the girl he would force himself to oblige...

Reluctantly he reached out and touched her large buttock, to the accompaniment of a sharp intake of breath from the girl. She spoke, but sounded a little nervous, as if she had changed her mind.

"I'm sorry," she murmured. "I'm forgetting. You must get out of your wet things. Come upstairs, you'll be tired." She headed for the locked door. 'My God, she doesn't waste her time,' he thought dejectedly. He nodded to the old woman, embarrassed, and then turned to face his entertainment for the evening.

77

The living room door was opened and he was again ushered out into the pitch black tunnel of the hall. In the dark he groped his way up the narrow stairs and wondered whether the lights were kept off because of the cost, or so that the men who came from the prison would never get to know the layout of the cottage. It seemed almost twice the size on the inside, he could just about make out several doors leading off the main landing.

He was soon to discover there was no electricity at all. When a lamp was finally lit he was so blinded by the flare of the match that he didn't even think to glance back out at the landing and stairs before the bedroom door slammed shut behind the girl. Shadows raced around the dark room like gathering spectres. When his eyes grew accustomed to the yellow glow emanating from the dusty flyblown oil lamp he remained facing the wall. He daren't look at the mound of flesh at his back; it would make the night impossible to carry through. He swallowed bile that had come into his throat.

"Take your things off," he heard her say, a command, while he was staring at the worn furniture and ancient metal double bed. There were no pictures on the whitewashed walls. The room had the atmosphere of a disused film set. "Come on then, take your wet things off," this time the voice was much more sensual, and despite himself he felt a tremor of excitement ripple through his body. It had been a long time since he'd felt the touch of a woman.

A pile of worn looking woollen nightwear had been thrown onto the bed, obviously for him to change into, but he didn't make a move to reach them until he heard the key turn in the lock. Spinning round he half opened his mouth to say "Don't go," but she hadn't. The door was locked from the inside, and just before he shut his eyes he had a glimpse of one of the most hideous female faces he thought he'd ever seen, a gargoyle made of flesh and bone bearing down on him like a living nightmare.

*   *   *

He wouldn't say that he woke up the next morning; he 'came to' as an unconscious man would. Blinking in the light of a miserable dawn that filtered through the small begrimed window. His body ached and his brain was fuddled. Something told him that he'd been sleeping with a horse on top of him, but when he looked around the dilapidated room he found himself alone. His old, faded prison clothes were draped over the back of a battered wicker chair.

Carefully easing himself out of bed he tried to get the bizarre dream he'd had into some sort of believable perspective. He'd dreamed that he'd been involved in a heavy petting session with a woman who, by rights, should have been in Madame Tussaud's Chamber of Waxwork Horrors. She was more animal than human, and she had been wild with passion...

But what really terrified him was that he'd *enjoyed it* – he had even wanted to go all the way – the sheer action had given him a surge of pleasure that he'd not felt since before he'd been detained at Her Majesty's Pleasure nearly a year ago. Maybe it really was true what they said about men being controlled by their loins... Shaking his head in wonder, he moved to get dressed, hissing through his teeth as his feet touched the stone-cold floorboards.

He was relieved at adorning the blue prison denim once more, it gave him a sense of normality. It was now dry, he didn't like to think how clean any other clothes offered to him might have been. 'Strange,' he thought, 'I'd never have said I'd be glad to get into these things again.' When he was fully clothed, and had checked to make sure that nothing was missing from his

79

pockets, he walked over to the window. After a great deal of straining at the rusted latch it swung it open. A breeze blew drizzle into his face, not as hard as yesterday's rain, but still dismal and irritating. It would soak through his dry clothes in a matter of minutes.

Glancing down he realised that he was at the back of the house, overlooking an untidy cobbled farmyard. A few small chickens were stalking around in the mud, and he caught the unmistakable aroma of pigs. His eyes moved to a large shed, and as he watched the door opened, revealing the nightmare that he'd just tried to forget. She carried a pail of steaming milk in each hand and once more had the appearance of being shapeless, helped by a tattered hooded rain cape that looked as though it was left over from the last war. Sensing that she was being stared at, she looked up, and her face split – a smile, he imagined.

"Hullo," came the smooth voice that didn't match the owner. Larry's brain began to work overtime. Perhaps she was a witch, a shape shifter; or maybe several shape shifters and the old woman didn't even exist. "Gran's cooking some breakfast. Come down, we've things to talk over." Good god; he almost reeled back from the window... 'things to talk over'; was it blackmail? Was he to be framed again? Had they even used protection last night? Was he to be held over a barrel for a fake pregnancy then shipped back to the prison, maybe even accused of rape?!

His stomach growled. Yes, he'd take them for the breakfast. Nothing more. Okay then, no bones about it last night had been, satisfying in a weird sort of way; but once he'd eaten he would bugger off as fast as his legs could carry him towards a more populated area. There had to be safer places to hide from the Old Bill.

Breakfast at the farm was one of the best meals that he'd consumed in his life. Whatever else the bent old lady was, she could certainly cook. Rasher upon rasher of tender bacon was spread over five perfectly fried eggs, which in turn nestled on three golden slices of fried home-baked bread. He'd not eaten an evening meal last night. He'd been too tired, especially after... he shuddered and tried to concentrate on the delicacies in front of him.

"Happen tha were't feshed, lad," cackled the old woman, who appeared to be attached to her armchair with superglue.

Judging by the unpleasant aroma emanating from that corner of the room she only moved from there when it was time to prepare a meal. He wondered when her clothes had last seen the inside of a washtub.

"I was rather hungry, yes," he replied, licking some grease from his lips. His eyes flicked to the living room door. Now, do it now while they're still uncertain of your actions. "I must thank you for your hospitality and go I'm afraid. I have put you to unnecessary risk sheltering me. I must get off before the police come here, it can only be a matter of time." He reached into his pocket and sorted three pound coins onto the table. Then he stood up to go.

A heavy hand on his shoulder gently pushed him back into his seat.

"No, not today," the soft voice turned his legs to rubber, whether from fear or arousal he no longer knew. "Give it 'til tomorrow, eh lad... or maybe a few days. Let the fuss die down. Besides, t'is raining cats and dogs again." Looking out through the fly-specked window nets he saw that she was right, and his heart sank. Drizzle he could have borne, but not the driving rain of yesterday. He was trapped. Also he was three pounds worse off. Having deposited the glinting coins on the table he couldn't very well pick them up again. The girl buried them in her giant fist and handed them to the crone who thanked him.

"Ta very much, lad. Tha's a gentleman if ever I saw'un. Better than t'others we've had, eh lass?"

The others; of course he'd forgotten that other jail breakers had been this way before him. These two must have a good system going, so he'd best fall in with their ways. Still he regretted the money; it could have bought him a decent train fair back down south...

"These others," he addressed himself to the old lady – it meant that he didn't have to look at the girl who had seated herself next to him. "These others; did they all get away?"

"Let's just say that t'police ne'er set eyes on them again." He missed the covert chuckle in the voice and was reassured.

"One more night pet," the voice whispered softly in his ear. He felt an overwhelming desire to lock himself in the out-house, but he remained resolute.

*   *   *

That day was spent indoors, walking around the small house, his senses delicately balanced between boredom, and the expectation of uniformed bodies bursting in at the door. The only times he ventured outside was to use the privy that stank quietly by itself near the dilapidated field fence. On one of these necessary trips he noticed a curious grassy hump at the back corner of the otherwise flat paddock. Long grass and bracken grew on it. When he questioned the girl she told him that it was very old and mysterious.

"One of them ancient burial mounds, it is. Folks here-abouts used to think it was the gateway to hell. Just a local legend mind. Got tongues wagging on a dark winter night I'll bet." This made him feel unsettled, but the green mound looked innocuous enough, so he dismissed it from his mind as an in-bred folk tale.

He tried to read as a distraction, but the books were all well-thumbed historical ones about unrequited love, and in such tiny print that they strained his eyes in the waning daylight of the cottage. Once he offered to help the girl with her chores, but she advised him to stay indoors as much as possible. The one thing that consoled him was the food. There was an abundance of it. Lunchtime brought roast pork, golden crackling, fresh peas and crisp roast potatoes washed down with the local beer, dark and heady. No wonder the girl was fat, for she ate twice as much as he did and the food was certainly very rich.

In contrast, the grandmother only gave herself a small helping, which she picked at and then deposited in the swill bucket. When tea came, with sticky fruitcake and crumpets saturated in lashings of melted butter, he had the vague feeling that he was being fattened up for something. A supper of cold meat, followed by fruit pie smothered in cream, confirmed his fears. The food was so moreish that he couldn't help but lick his plate clean. He ate alone at the table, the lump of a girl choosing to eat sitting hunched over in a broken easy-chair.

As soon as he was done the grandmother cleared the table and disappeared upstairs. He figured out what was going on when the girl appeared, carrying two mugs of warm mulled ale. At least, he assumed it was the girl. She looked totally different and he wondered for a second if it was the same person. Perhaps the lamplight and the beer were playing tricks on him. This girl was beautiful, not supermodel 'pretty'; even the sympathetically cut dress couldn't hide her bulk. Yet she was somewhat of a curvaceous pin-up model, all shapely and alluring, despite her size.

She'd bathed and washed her hair, which now shone a silky brunette in the soft yellow glow from the lamps. Her face was the most striking part of the metamorphosis. Careful and experienced use of make-up had transformed it from a pasty lump of dough into a mature – even intelligent – sculpture. A strong odour of lavender filled the room and he took the hot ale from her in a daze.

"You're... it's... how did you...?" He gasped.

"Yes, we can let our hair down occasionally in these wild northern wastes. Cheers," she said demurely.

He drank deeply, a warm feeling suffusing his body, he couldn't take his eyes off the transformed girl.

"Look," she continued quietly. "I'm sorry about last night, but..."

"No, no, please don't apologise; it was just as much my fault. I'm sorry I was so... Well, I'm sorry I misjudged you. Your hospitality has been faultless." She smiled.

"You must be wondering what someone like me is doing in a dump like this. Wearing such... worn clothes."

"A bit cliched isn't it?" he said, taking another draught. His eyes began to soak up the lamplight as the strong drink pervaded his brain. "Cliched but true, I've been thinking about it a lot. I couldn't help question why you and the old lady are here alone."

"Well, I wasn't always this... 'big', you know;" she indicated her rolling body with her hands, running the palms over her clothes seductively. "Gran does rather feed me up."

"She's a superb cook." It was an honest response. The girl, now a voluptuous woman, sighed heavily and looked into the flickering lamp light.

"Yes, unfortunately she is... I used to be a magazine model actually, in London... a while back now. Had the pick of the boys down there, and did my share of night clubbing. Concerts... bars..." He eyed her up and down, trying to make out the former fashion model trapped within the large frame.

"So why give it all up?" He asked quickly. She turned to him, deflated.

"Well, I'm not proud to admit that I was conned – by Gran of all people, the old bag..." She put her hands on the table and he noticed that she was wearing bright red nail varnish, expertly applied. "My own flesh and blood. I'm sorry to be so forward, does that shock you?"

He laughed, relaxed already.

"No not really. From what I've seen she's not the kind of person I would normally associate with in a social sense... she seems quite," he searched for an appropriate word. "Canny; a bit fly. No offence meant." The girl giggled. It was husky and low. She took another sip of her drink.

"None taken. She's lived here all her life, on the farm. She used to employ a staff of ten when she was younger. They all left or caused her hassle and she shopped them in to the local Bobby. Then I had a spot of bother... a stupid, *stupid,* unwanted pregnancy..."

Larry leaned forward, she was being so candid, and now she was clean, eloquent, her voice matched her looks. He felt extremely attracted to her.

"... I just couldn't get any work after that; plus it was a bit of a scandal with my parents. So, she asked me up here until it all blew over. Just to pitch in and learn some life-skills." He let the information settle in his inebriated mind.

"But where's the..." There was a silence, the lamp light flickered and crackled. The girl sighed.

"Oh, *that.* It died at birth. Thank God. Can you imagine bringing up a child here in this hovel?" Silence filled the gaps in the room like tar. "I'm all Granny's got now. When she goes this will be mine..." She looked around the room, it was a fair size and the structure of the cottage seemed sound. With the land and the out buildings it could be worth quite a bit. The girl smiled wistfully.

"...Trouble is, I've been here close on seven years, and she still won't shuffle off this bloody mortal coil. I often hoped one of the prisoners would come here and bash her in just so this nightmare can be over..." He found himself shocked by her forthrightness, but he was letting his guard down. For the first time since he arrived yesterday he was shutting off his awareness. Her eyes stared at him darkly and he wanted to leap into them, to have her all to himself. "When this farm is mine I shall sell up and move back down south as fast as possible. To tell the truth, I sometimes think the only thing that keeps me sane is the men who come from the prison..." Larry could barely contain himself, it was like some sick script from a film. He'd been snared by an evil witch who then turned out to be a beauty in disguise. He watched her sipping at the warm ale, hanging on her every word.

"...Mind you," she stroked the back of his hand, and he hurriedly put down his mug. "They're not all like *you*. I felt like turning a lot of them in, taking them back to the jail myself like. But I didn't. I let them have their way with me then pointed them in the direction of the best escape route... It was the right thing to do." He could control himself no longer, as she had planned. Their lips gently touched, the beer, lamplight and perfume drove the last vestiges of caution from his mind.

*   *   *

When he awoke, he could see that it was later than planned by the thin watery sunlight that came in through the window of the girl's bedroom. The magic of last night still lingered, but he wasn't surprised by the dinginess of his surroundings. He'd awoken in this bed for the past few mornings and knew the room intimately. Larry groaned inwardly. That first morning he'd felt good, ready to take on the world. Had even thought about staying there of his own accord. Recharge the old batteries; build himself up after twelve months of that ghastly gruel they called prison food. He could have even put up with the hideous daytime looks of the girl. But now he was spent.

The good food and rest that filled his daylight hours could not boost his ardour for the long passionate nights. It was several days in a row now. Last night he'd only just managed it. Yes, the girl was great, but not *every* night. Surely she had to sleep some time... That was why

86

this morning, as she was dressing, he'd asked her if they could give it a miss for a while.

"Yes my love," she had replied. "Of course. Why didn't you say so before?" He'd drifted off to sleep again, but had now been aroused by what had sounded like the bedroom door closing. When he looked there was no one there.

Leisurely he dressed, and felt in his pocket for his cigarettes – gone. All his possessions were gone save for his handkerchief and matches. Shit, it couldn't have been the girl – must have been that thieving old hag of a grandmother, taking the opportunity whilst he was asleep. He'd never really trusted her. If she'd wanted money he could have given her a fiver, but... He'd had twenty saved up in there and she'd taken the lot, as well as all his loose change for public transport!

Opening the door he went downstairs to look for the girl. Guessing that she'd be feeding the chickens he made for the front door to walk around the edge of the building, but hurriedly dived into the living room when there came a loud knock and a deep male voice.

"Mrs Kettlewell, are you there? Come on ma'am, it's the police. We want a word."

"Alright, alright, I'm a'coming!" Came a screech from upstairs. Shit, shit, shit, he'd done it again; allowed himself to be trapped. He couldn't trust the old lady, and where was he to hide in a house this small! He looked around the living room; there were no tall cupboards, nothing to conceal his body in the slightest.

Quietly he crawled over to the side window of the room, and then fell backwards in alarm when it squeaked open, seemingly of its own accord. A familiar face appeared.

"Hey, Larry, are you in there?"

"Yes," he replied, shaking. He noticed how her hair glowed in the morning sun. A memory of burying his face in that deep forest of brown calmed him.

"Quick then my dear, come with me. T'is only one policeman at the moment. We still have time." He crawled back to the open window, and she reached in, more or less hauling him out onto the muddy cobbles of the farmyard.

"Someone's pinched all my money..." Larry whispered loudly, frantically. The girl ignored him.

"Hush," she said, taking his arm, "tell me later!"

"Where are we going?" he asked as quietly as possible, his breath making clouds of steam in the freezing air. "The barn would be a good shout? I can hide behind the pigs."

"No, in cases like this we have something much better. A real safe spot at t'edge of the paddock." Her voice had gone back to its local lilt; it filled him with apprehension. Where was her London charm? If only he could hear a southerner's voice it would give him hope.

He half walked, half tripped behind her across the damp uneven ground.

"The privy?" He asked in desperation. She laughed quietly, chastising him.

"No, silly, the burial mound. It's got it's own door." He felt a chill fall over him. He had completely forgotten that lump of mud in the paddock was anything more than a rubble heap.

"What? Didn't you call it '*the gateway to hell*'?" He was doubtful. Uneasy. There were much better places to secret themselves.

"Yes, you'll soon see. Don't fret, It's where we put all the others when the law comes. You'll be safe there too." Larry looked back towards the farm house.

The old woman's shrill voice was heard calling the girl's name from the front step.

"Hurry, there isn't time to argue now. You'll not be seen there, I promise. Safe as houses." They jogged across the back paddock to the mound, bending low to the grass as they went. The girl scrabbled on her knees in the long weeds until she found a large brass ring, tarnished with age. Tugging at this brought away a thick clod of turf, she swore as it caught her finger, revealing a huge stone that seemed to serve as a door. Underneath the slab was a dark hole, from which an unpleasant smell drifted up.

It was like the stink of an old meat safe he had once encountered at the back of a butcher's yard. He assumed the mound was used as a make-shift shed for storing animal feed when the barn was full, they did have a lot of pigs, and a few goats too...

"In... there?" he hesitated. There came another, more insistent, call from the house. The girl was looking around, she seemed genuinely panicked for him.

"It's our only chance my love! Look, it won't be for long. I just can't bear the thought of them taking you away from me!" Larry felt slightly more assured. "You can't open it from the inside, so don't fret, but I'll be back in about half an hour when we've got rid of the police – I promise I'll be as quick as I can."

Larry looked back to the house, expecting to see the policeman turn the corner into the farm yard at any moment. He wondered how many more years he'd get on his sentence for escaping and evading capture.

"But I -" he started to protest.

"There's no time!" she whispered, and kissed him hard on the lips, remnant of lavender oil and make-up filling his senses. In a split second she apologised and shoved him bodily into the hole with such a force he was winded, his chest felt like he'd been hit with a steam train piston!

He fell about ten feet onto what he imagined was a pile of sticks and glanced up, his head spinning. He was righted just in time to see a last whirling patch of daylight, and the silhouette of the girl, then the stone door thumped shut. He was alone, in total blackness and silence.

As he lay panting in the cold hole, trying to get his breath back, he was able to think clearly for the first time that morning. Why had the police only come to check now, yet he'd been gone nearly a week? Surely this farm would have been one of their first ports of repeat call; in fact, she had told him so. Probably checking twice in case he'd slipped the net.

And why only one policeman? Looking for someone of his 'calibre' and his perceived crimes, surely they would have sent at least two squad cars and dogs too... He picked himself up slowly, not liking the idea that had formed in his mind.

The hiding place really stank.

It must have been hollowed out for use as a storehouse originally by the first people to farm the land. It was so small, barely a room at all. Coughing, he wondered if there was a good air supply with the door shut and covered in earth. He went to take a careful pace forward but tripped over what he assumed to be another bundle of sticks. Then he remembered his matches – the only bit of personal property he'd been able to snatch up from the bedroom. He took out the box, and struck up a light. For an instant he was blinded by the flare, but as the flame settled down, he was shocked into a brutal understanding of where he was.

It was indeed the gateway to hell. In the steady glow of the match he found himself in a stone room full of human remains: skeletons; decomposing bodies; unrecognisable bones, long separated from their wisened ligaments by age.

The match went out.

Stunned, sickened he lit another.

Mouths hung open in sinister smiles, as the dried skin curled back from yellowing teeth. Dark sockets betrayed no sign of the long-shrivelled eyeballs. And all the bodies had one thing in common – faded blue prison uniforms. Oh yes, these were 'the others' all right, and the police had never set eyes on them again, true enough! Unaware of the warm liquid that ran down his legs he tried to count how many there were, but the match burnt his fingers and the thick, suffocating darkness returned.

Then Larry screamed.

He screamed and screamed until the air ran out.

THE WORM

He paused, and then hesitantly drew back, uncertain of what to do next. The creature opposite was still crouched in the same menacing position, but the cries (half angry, half frightened), were reduced to nonsensical growling. It was beginning to dribble.

Sir Guy was not versed in the skills of doctoring, but he could recognise genuine madness when he came across it, and this pitiful beast was certainly insane. In the flickering light from the torch that crackled in a rusting bracket on the wall, the dark wheals on wrist and neck marked the festering wounds caused by the cruel iron manacles.

Sir Guy of Welbury had penetrated the reeking darkness of the dungeon as soon as his men had broken through the gates of the castle. He had been appalled at the filth and squalor of the cells below. The antediluvian gaoler and his heavy club had proved no match for keen steel; even now the rats were feeding on the blood that oozed from his freshly severed head.

Desperately, Sir Guy had searched each cell, knowing full well that his men would not be able to hold the castle for long. His journey through this labyrinth of neglect and deprivation was marked by a crescendo of slamming doors, rising to intensity as each room revealed its long-concealed horrors. He couldn't find his friend Sir Geoffrey anywhere. His rescue was the sole reason for this foolhardy assault! Finally Sir Guy had come to this stinking hole with its green streaming walls, and a floor so soiled that even the plague rats avoided it.

As he burst through a rotten door, that one hard blow with a mailed fist was enough to splinter, a grubby pile of rags in one corner twitched itself into a sitting

92

position. Sir Guy had stared at the prisoner in horror, sheer disgust, as he hurriedly flung his sword to the floor. He carefully removed the manacles that felt rough as nutmeg graters, all the while being subjected to a torrent of unintelligible abuse from the man, the creature.

Was this even the right place? Sir Geoffrey de Banmar had been, if not tall, dashing; a real man for the ladies... Some would say over-polite, but he could tell a ribald story as well as the next fellow... and he had taken particular pride in his dress, the ornamentation on his armour being flamboyant rather than practical. If this was the same man, then God have mercy on his tortured soul. One ear was missing, the hair and beard were matted with fetid slime, and when the man opened his mouth Sir Guy noted that his tongue had been slit! Half his teeth were gone through decay, leaving red raw gums behind.

Over and over the brave rescuer tried to tell his old friend who he was, but the man had lost all reason. Judging by what he was throwing at the knight saviour, all sense of human decency too. With a surprisingly quick movement for one so wasted (almost as though it was the carrying through of a long thought out plan), the now free prisoner snatched a knife from Sir Guy's belt and slashed at his rescuer's surcoat. The heavy material parted like butter, and the blade bit deep into the leather underneath.

The knight jumped back and aimed an instinctive blow, but the lunatic had retreated, whimpering, into the corner where he crouched. He started growling and dribbling again, his hand weaving a continual dance with the knife. It was as if he was trying to hypnotise a snake. Sir Guy hesitated only long enough to ask God's forgiveness, and then dived below the slicing blade. He grasped his sword tight, closed his eyes, and thrust upwards with both hands. There came an ear splitting shriek, and a thin fountain of warm blood spurted into his face. Turning his back on the still twitching body he wiped his sword on his already dirtied surcoat. He couldn't even bring himself to retrieve his knife. It was over.

Returning to the equally dim corridor, he was halted in his tracks by the nearing sound of shouting, and the metallic clash of swords. Three of his men were backing down the passageway, hampered by its narrowness, desperately trying to fight off an equally handicapped band of foot soldiers. Sir Guy moved to rush forward and swing his sword, but by this time the enemy had halted, held up by general uncertainty and a number of corpses blocking the way, slumped against the oozing green stone walls.

Taking their opportunity, Sir Guy and his comrades ran deeper into the honeycomb of the dungeons, through places where few torches were ever lit, and where one or two slow gaolers proved no match for the adept swordsmen. Finally they rested in a dank, rotting cell. Its contents revealed by only a single sputtering torch that one of them had hastily grabbed a few minutes before. Even this poor orange flame threatened to be extinguished at any moment as it was battered by a subterranean breeze that wafted strange, nauseating odours around the tunnels.

Whilst catching his breath, Sir Guy tried to encourage their thoughts about what the next course of action should be. They felt that they had already run for miles. Was this just a vast maze of tunnels, riddling the inside of the hill like worm holes in an apple, or had they been running in circles? Not one corridor remained straight for very long, and each cell looked much like another – although there were some small differences in the way they were lit; the number of torches had been steadily diminishing.

One of the men in a quest for more light, wandered as far away as he dared, carefully feeling the walls. Even a snuffed torch could be rekindled. Anyway, more light would tell the rough position of... A short scream brought the other three out into the main tunnel in time to see their companion stagger forward into their torchlight and collapse face down into the sodden mush that covered the floor. Protruding from his back, glinting dully in the yellow flame, was a small jewel-encrusted dagger.

They tensed, ears straining, but all they could catch was the sound of distant laughter, and the soft clatter of retreating footsteps. Sir Guy knelt and removed the weapon. The two other men moved forward to inspect it as best they could in the quivering light.

"That's no ordinary dagger," ventured Lionel, Sir Guy's squire, "It must surely belong to some lord." The other man, Cedric, a sergeant, peered closely at the embellished hilt.

"Aye, it has letters on it." The knight held it close to the flame, and traced two interlaced characters with his finger.

D. C.

"So," Sir Guy said after a pause. "We are indeed pursued by important persons. This blade must belong to Sir Dunstan Corvester himself. A personal message delivered to us, I fancy. No other guard would be given the opportunity to use such a weapon. Well, I have a life to settle with him now."

"It would seem, sir, that he has several more lives to settle with you too," muttered Lionel. The breeze from the corridor felt unearthly. Chilled.

"Hmmm," Sir Guy hooked the dagger into his leather belt. "I shall return this at the right time, and in the appropriate manner. How went the battle up above... as if I couldn't guess the answer."

"We were forced to retreat sooner than we wished," replied Cedric. "Our fatalities are probably light, but I am thinking there must be many wounded. Corvester brought up extra bowmen we were not prepared for."

"We are almost certainly the only ones inside the castle now," added Lionel tentatively.

"You ever were a comfort to me, Lionel. We must get away from this place, it is... unsafe..." replied Sir Guy, meaning the corridor.

"Aye my lord, there must be a way out somewhere," agreed Lionel, referring to the situation.

"What are you thinking, brave sir?" Asked Cedric, unsure what either of them meant.

"If you will stay with me, men," said Sir Guy, knowing that there was no other choice, "I mean to have my revenge on his lordship Corvester."

"And if we three don't stay, if we try to make for the surface?" asked Lionel, his voice wavering slightly.

"Together we might have a chance – apart we are certain to be picked off, or go mad wandering in these God forsaken tunnels... and for another, I mean to have my revenge either way. Do as you will." The wind moaned eerily and the men shivered beneath their mail.

"May I suggest that we first try and gather in a supply of torches," said Cedric, after a prolonged silence. "I for one would wish to see any weapon aimed at me in time defend myself."

*   *   *

The first rays of a mild spring sun penetrated the small, unglazed, window of Sir Dunstan Corvester's bedchamber as he slowly awoke from a troubled sleep. Despite his exhaustion after yesterday's battle, despite his victory, despite his *relish* at having Welbury legitimately at his mercy (for had not Sir Guy launched an unprovoked attack on him?), despite all of these things his slumbers had been haunted by lurid dreams of dragons, and beasts from the dark realm of Hades.

Once, when he could have sworn that he was awake, he had heard a distant, blood-chilling, ululation, as though some fiend from hell was thrashing about deep inside the hill on which the castle stood. Involuntarily his mind conjured up memories of childhood stories about Lords of the castle who had mysteriously disappeared 'below'. He'd always assumed that the tales were told to keep him away from the meandering labyrinth that had been dug out of the rock many centuries before; but now he wasn't so sure...

Anyway, *what of it!* He'd ignored the youthful admonitions, and had set up his great subterranean 'hostelry', as he was pleased to call it.
"Once a guest," he would say, "you will never wish to leave." Which was true. The waking death, however long and painful, seemed to satisfy his claim... He blinked once or twice, and then opened his eyes. As he stared at the nubile girl sleeping next to him he listened for any stirrings within the mighty stone fortress. Below, in the courtyard, a guard coughed; otherwise silence.

Wondering whether it was worth asking the girl's name he rolled onto his back and roughly shook her. Groaning, she shielded her eyes against the early daylight. "Girl," he rasped, God's teeth his mouth felt foul and dry. "*Girl*, get back to the kitchens now, be gone." At the same time he gave her a hefty push, and she slid ungracefully onto the cold wooden floor, whence she gathered up her clothes and padded sleepily out of the sparsely furnished room. Not for the first time.

*   *   *

97

Cedric awoke suddenly, and his eyes snapped open. In the fitful light of a guttering torch he could see Lionel sleeping, half sitting, huddled against the damp wall of the small cell. Of Sir Guy there was no sign. Slightly worried, but unsurprised, Cedric yawned and stiffly got to his feet. His body felt like someone had driven two ploughing oxen over it. The cold and damp atmosphere was eating into his very soul. Carefully he lit another torch from the dying embers of the first. Something had woken him, and not his master by the look of it. He reluctantly decided that he'd better find out what it was.

In the tiny doorway he bumped headlong into a running figure. The knight spoke at once, trying to catch his breath at the same time.

"Come Cedric, we must move again! They are nearly up with us. Wake Lionel immediately." The young squire was already on his feet. "I want to get to an area where the walls do not play tricks on our ears," continued Sir Guy. "Here, we are in a dead spot. We'll never hear them coming!"

"But that noise, that howl..." began Cedric.

"It woke me too I am sure! At first I believed it to be part of a dream, yet I am glad that it was real and so loud, for otherwise we would be dead men! Move! Move!"

A dark shape rushed into the torchlight and thrust a sword at the back of Welbury's neck. With a speed that he felt incapable of, Cedric countered the thrust with a mailed fist and punched his other hand into the assailant's groin. Sir Guy threw himself sideways and brought his weapon down on the back of the man's head, cleaving his unprotected skull clean in two.

"We are caught! You check the way ahead, sir," cried Cedric, "Lionel and I will hold these curs back!" Without hesitating Sir Guy swept up and lit another torch, then sped off down a dark side tunnel. As he did so, another of those awful cries echoed around the empty passageways.

He was joined seconds later by his squire and sergeant. Both were unharmed yet uneasy.

"There don't seem to be any more, sir," said Cedric.

"Either that or that awful sound has scared them off," added Lionel.

"It would scare me off too," replied Welbury,"if I had anywhere else to go... But I suspect this is Corvester using tricks of the mind to unnerve us. Come, this way." He said with a confidence he didn't feel, because he was struck by the fear that they were heading towards the source of that demonic wail, and there was no turning back.

*　　　*　　　*

Sir Dunstan Corvester yawned, stretched lazily, and then leisurely slid from his bed. Struggling into his undershirt, he pulled on warm woollen socks and wandered over to the window. He looked out. The courtyard had been cleared from most of the litter of the battle. Rust red patches still stained the scuffed soil, but otherwise the only memorial to Welbury's attack was a small heap of stripped corpses against one wall near the main gate. These were to be buried later in the day. The heavy carcass he sought was conspicuous by its absence.

Corvester was about to turn away from the window when something moved down in the deliberately 'nondescript' entrance to the dungeons. Interested, he leaned his elbows on the rough stone sill and watched. Into the morning light came two men. One was heavily supported by the other, and both had ominous crimson gashes on their faces. The stronger of the two blinked in the sunlight. His companion was doubled up with pain.

"You there!" Sir Dunstan was curious, he called to them. "Have you been brawling?" The upright man raised his eyes to the window.

"No, my lord. There are still at least three of Welbury's men alive down below in the tunnels."

"What!" He bellowed in response.

Heated anger welled up. Had he not buried his dagger in Welbury's own back? Though it *was* very dark down there... The injured soldier slumped even more.

"Sir, one of them appears to be Welbury himself." A hideous scowl moulded itself onto Corvester's face, and an imperceptible twitch began contorting the skin under his right eyelid.

"Are they being... *dealt with*?" He barked.

"We're trying Lord, but they're running deeper into the tunnels and dungeons. It's very difficult to fight in the narrow corridors."

"Idiots," he muttered to himself, and he felt a prickle of apprehension across his back.

If he had to go down there again, he wanted to stay as close to the daylight as possible. He leaned right out of the window.

"You go back down there and tell my men if they can't take or kill Welbury, then at least stop him getting deeper. Even I don't know where all those blasted tunnels go to!"

The man motioned to his injured burden with his free hand.

"But sir, what about...?" The soldier indicated his slumped partner.

"Leave him, man. Can't you see he's dead?"

*   *   *

100

There were no spare torches.

He lit the last from the dying embers of its brother, and as it spat into a strong yellow incandescence he tried to pierce the gloom ahead.

The darkness was an impenetrable wall.

There was no comforting pinprick of light signifying a way out onto the hillside or back into the castle grounds. He would settle now for a tunnel that would take them back out into the castle proper, even though it would be bristling with guards... Knowing that to wish was pointless, he still found himself hoping that they'd pick up more torches; apart from anything else the need for light may have also hampered their pursuers. If he went further and took this last burning brand, he would leave his two comrades floundering around in a darkness so complete that it wasn't even black.

No, he couldn't allow those faithful souls to fall victim to the motley band of cut-throats who probably knew this labyrinth like the backs of their hands. Equally he would leave no man – except perhaps Corvester – to wander blindly in the suffocating gloom until starvation, or madness, would take its toll. He still had his honour, and there was a code to follow.

Stealthily he crept back up the passage and disappeared into one of the smaller side turnings, his sword drawn and ready. Seconds later two shadowy figures rushed past with a guttering torch between them, and ducked into another side way. Sir Guy eased himself from his hiding place and cautiously made his way after the men, yet there was no sign of their torch now... Was it being sheltered, was its carrier farther ahead than expected, or had it been extinguished?

Suddenly a rough hand that smelled anything but clean was clamped over his mouth and nose. He felt a steel point tickle his neck under his ear.

"Hold!" hissed a familiar voice at the back of his head. "Stand, or you are a *dead man*."

"Cedric," said another voice, "one day you will get us into great trouble." Welbury was released as though a trap had been sprung.

"My liege, I am sorry." He shook hands with the knight, and all three sheathed their swords.

"Found any more torches?" asked Sir Guy.

"Only what you have, this one is spent." replied Lionel. "We could try and go back to get some from the last cells, but I don't even know where 'back' is any more."

"Well, then this is the last of them. By my reckoning we have about two hours of light left to us. How far behind you were Corvester's guards?"

"It is hard to say, sir," said Cedric, "I am not certain if we *are* that far away from where we began, yet as much as I would guess... we don't seem to have recrossed our steps. We'd best continue."

"Aye, lord," added Lionel the youngest of the three. "It can't be long before we reach the side of the hill. I have faith in that. Maybe a hollow or a collection of boulders disguise the exit out there and that's why we've yet to see a source of daylight."

"So your advice is that we strike out once more, and don't try to return. Is that it?" Asked Cedric hesitantly. In the shadowy light Sir Guy nodded.

As if to give a verbal answer distant sound of shouts and running feet echoed from the granite walls in the distance at their back. But at the same time a stale odour of rotting meat, unlike any they had yet encountered, washed over them. Aside from suppressing their growing hunger, this made each man view the darkness ahead with a fear that he had never felt before. They almost turned to fight, and end it there, but their

102

bodies acted from years of battle experience and they found themselves moving on swiftly down the tunnel, keeping within the light of their final crackling torch flame. At least this way they may have some time to regain their strength before another encounter.

About a hundred yards further they came upon a yawning hole in the passage floor which, on closer inspection, revealed a flight of steps that disappeared into a darkness somehow different from the rest. It was colder – icy, compared with the stifling narrow tunnels they'd so far suffered beyond the dungeons. Perhaps it was a way out... Perhaps it led downwards to an underground river which was the cause of the occasional breeze that touch their faces.

*   *   *

Corvester was growing impatient. Still no news of a death. *The death*. If his men were led any deeper into the hill, probably half of them wouldn't come back. Was that the plan? Was Welbury even actually in there... Yes, he had seen him... but, supposing it was all a complicated plot? Welbury may have split his forces, persuaded a small group of men to take their chances in the tunnels on the understanding that Corvester's followers would be lost underground, while Welbury overwhelmed the castle with the main part of his army.

Here Sir Dunstan had over-estimated his foe. Corvester for all his faults was a brilliant planner and tactician; hence the fact that he had remained at large for so long. Welbury was a man of heart; he couldn't even win a game of chess against a decent player... Worry pushed Sir Dunstan to make a hasty decision. Despite his fear of the dark labyrinth, he would have to lead the operation himself. Taking several deep draughts of wine (to calm the sudden fit of the shakes that came upon him), he donned his leather hauberk, selected a good sword, and set off for the dungeons.

*   *   *

The prospect of entering that cold, inhospitable, inky-black, abyss was daunting to the three desperate warriors. The stone steps were spread with a dark green slime, almost like seaweed, and a small trickle of water dripped down the centre where it had carved a smooth channel for itself. Despite a raging thirst, no one stooped to drink. They were hopeful that it was indeed a path to a river, or brook. The algae certainly gave that impression, as did the small spring that was feeding the dripping water.

The rising odour, which was now definitely recognisable as the stink of putrid flesh, had become so strong that Lionel's eyes began to water. Each man felt his empty stomach twist into a knot of terror as they prepared to enter the hole. Something touched Lionel's back, and he jumped, giving an instinctive yelp. A gruff voice spoke, but it was a voice that lacked much of its usual hard resolution.

"Do not attempt to reach your weapon, knave. I have no wish to be the cause of an easy demise at this *precise* moment, but I will run you through if it is found to be necessary."

"Corvester!" Sir Guy exclaimed in disgust. Had he been of the peasantry he would have spat. "How came you here?"

"I must congratulate you, Welbury," Corvester raised his torch as high as he could to glare at the other's torn and dishevelled appearance. "You have managed to occupy a large number of my men. You were easy to reach... I merely followed the chain of wounded souls."

Out of the corner of his eye, Sir Dunstan saw Cedric's hand reach towards his sword.

"Move any further sergeant, and I will skewer your..." The rest of the words were lost as Lionel viciously brought his heel into contact with Corvester's shin. Momentarily caught off guard, he staggered back a step. Cedric grabbed Corvester's torch, the squire dropped to his knees. It was merely a slight movement on Welbury's part to push the unbalanced body of Corvester down the steep, slippery, bone splintering, steps into the darkness. A not too distant cry bounced down the passage towards the trio and they swung the torch on all sides, checking for the knight's personal guard.

Without further ado, Sir Guy spoke firmly.

"We go down too. If only to be sure he has perished." The brave knight led the way with his failing torch. He was followed by Lionel. Cedric, clutching the other torch from Corvester, brought up the rear a few paces behind. They were alert, ears and eyes darting back and forth for any sign of movement that wasn't a guttering shadow. Forty five uneven, weed-slimed, steps brought them to the beginning of another corridor that sloped down into impenetrable gloom. The foul wind touched them once more, there was no scent of woodland or fresh air.

"What *is this*?" grunted Cedric in surprise. "Witchcraft?" And it did seem like that, for of Sir Dunstan Corvester's body there was no sign. There was nowhere he could have fled to after the injuries he sustained on the steps. They had all heard bones cracking. A heavy thud. He surely must have been there at the base, unconscious, or mortally wounded, if not dead.

"I don't like this," muttered Lionel, crossing himself, and coughing with the strengthening ungodly odour. "We'd best go back and fight in the corridors above... or even give ourselves up to their mercy..." his courage was failing fast.

"What *mercy* would you receive were Corvester still alive? A cell in one of these infernal tunnels... if you were lucky. No, a whole army awaits us up there ready to pounce. We would never see daylight again." But even Sir Guy found that his legs were reluctant to move further forward, even with the aid of both the torches.

"Well, I say go on," said Cedric stoically. He was a large man, afraid of little, and he preferred deeds to thought – mainly because he didn't think very quickly. "Sir Dunstan Corvester is somewhere about here, and we should catch up with him very easily, for after a tumble like that he is sure to be severely wounded." So saying, he gripped his sword and set off at a brisk march down the tunnel, his torch (taken from Corvester) casting a warm orange glow on the soaking wet stone walls. These were not walls made by masons, these were hewn from the rock of the hill itself.

The other two looked on uneasily after him for a while, and were only spurred forward when the yellow flame of his torch suddenly sputtered and died.
"Cedric!"
"Sir Guy...!" His voice sounded different, hesitant, as if trying to push down a rising panic. When he continued, the sergeant was whining like a fearful child. "Sir, your torch... *give me your torch*... hurry, sir, it's touching me -"
The sentence ended with an inhuman roar, which rapidly diminished to a choking gurgle. Welbury was just about to shout in response when he heard a fearsome, evil, sound. It was the most loathsome noise had ever pervaded his ears: a guzzling, slavering, sucking interspersed with a dull tearing sound and the wet crack of bone. It was like listening to a mad dog ripping a rabbit to shreds, only sounding much louder within the rocky confines of the tunnel!

No wonder there had been not a sign of Corvester. Lionel stood rooted to the spot.

"Lionel, back to the stairs! Hurry! I will fight this thing if I must, to avenge Cedric and protect you!" The young man's eyes grew wide with terror.

"No, no my lord! I cannot go back in the dark. I – I will hold the last torch for you! I am your squire after all!"

"Thank you," Sir Guy envied Lionel his visible fear. As a knight he must be strong in case his tale was to be told for generations. The knight had to fight his impulse to run, otherwise all was lost, and his reputation would be for ever deemed cowardly.

They edged their way slowly down the passage towards the gruesome sounds. Then, into the torchlight, came a thing that made even the battle-hardened Welbury choke. If Lionel had had any food in his stomach he would have vomited. He spat a mouthful of bile. A hideous being, the upper half almost man – but with a grotesque parody of a head twice the normal size – the lower half scaly, slimy, worm. The top of the skull was crowned by a few matted tufts of what looked like human hair. An almost visible stench oozed from its bloodstained jaws. Its lips were smeared with a reddish froth, and tattered shreds of what must have been... Cedric. Corvester's ripped shirt also hung from the ill spaced, pointed, teeth.

This *thing* moved close to the wall, as if for comfort; like a blind man feels his way around a strange room. Its arms were shapeless, vestigial almost, but they were ever moving, like the antennae of an insect. It slithered nearer. A vast pulsating slug. The only sound was of rasping breath. The torchlight showed the skin to be a vile olive colour, with glistening pink patches of what could have been raw flesh, as though it had grazed itself with continual rubbing on the rough, damp, rock.

It stopped, and lifted a pair of lidless eyes. They were black, and full of malevolent hate towards the two men. Then for a second its expression altered, softened almost. A fearful... no, a pleading look came over the face, and it uttered a strangled, gurgling, howl, which formed itself into the tortured words;

"Help... me..." Welbury's jaw dropped with the stunned surprise of recognition.

"Cor- Corvester...?" His lips silently framed the word. Lionel could no longer contain the incredible panic that was bubbling through his body. Without a thought for anything but his own life, he fled back towards the stairs, leaving Sir Guy in total darkness with the abomination.

"Lionel! In the name of God, bring me a light!"

Something touched his knee. In desperation he hacked about with his sword, raising a couple of squeals, then he sliced straight into his own shin. As he buckled he already felt, but could not see, the ripping teeth at work on his feet. Despite the agony he fought to free his blade from where it was wedged in his own leg bone. Waves of pain so intense that he was numbed to them swept over his lower body. Then a greater anguish engulfed him.

Lionel threw himself at the steps, moaning unintelligibly. Time and again he slid on the slick green weed, bruising and grazing himself, ripping his fingernails in a bid to find purchase. Halfway up the torch fell from his grasp, but he found that he didn't need it. There was light in the corridor above! Dear God, salvation! Tears running down his cheeks, reciting the words of the 'Hail Mary' over and over again, he struggled upwards...

*   *   *

The two guards waiting at the top of the steps drew back. They had heard the various sounds from below, and were not certain what it was that was now noisily scrabbling up to meet them. They poised, tensed, ready for action. A shadowy figure appeared in the torchlight, it erupted from the hole and rushed straight at them! One of the men swung his sword with all his might. The young squire's body ran a few more paces and then crumpled into a broken heap, while the head of the boy bounced back down the steps into the all-consuming darkness.

There was silence.

Cautiously the two men approached the hole.

Still nothing. They relaxed. Still nothing. Lionel's killer cleaned his sword, and began to talk quietly to his companion as they walked away.

Guided by the flickering light, the worm slithered closer.

THE HOLIDAY COTTAGE

1979, South-West Cornwall

When he stepped on to the small gravel driveway he knew that something was different. It was the feeling one gets on a sunny day when you know that it's going to rain and, sure enough, by lunchtime the grey clouds are spreading thick and fast. It was a knowledge that had begun to form in his mind as the holiday cottage appeared through the dusty windscreen of his car when they returned from a brief shopping expedition. His new wife struggled with two bulging bags of purchases, and he rushed to help her as she eased herself between the closed wooden garage door and the back of the car.

"I don't know why you couldn't just ask the owners for a key for that thing," she said laughingly. "Married three days and already I'm doing all the hard work!" He made a vague reply and took one of the carrier bags from her. "What's up?" She continued, "you look as though you've seen a ghost." Instead of making some wisecrack about her 'haunting eyes', he just stared at her with a peculiar expression on his face. He felt odd. "Oh Jon," she squeezed his arm reassuringly. "Don't be silly. The company wouldn't let out the cottage if it was haunted. I was only joking."

Yes, she was right. Here he was, Jonathan Minton, with his lovely wife on their lovely honeymoon. They had been able to rent a postcard-worthy 17th century cottage from Picturesque Holidays, a reputable tourist firm in London. Yet all he could think of on that swelteringly hot June day was ghosts. Too much sun, he reasoned with himself. Too much sun and an incredibly long drive down to Cornwall earlier in the day.

Before stepping through the low front door surrounded by pink scented roses, he took another look at the small house. For just a second the windows seemed to distort, as though the glass had become warped and pitted, but in an instant the reflections of the trees from across the road shone out as sharply as they had always done. He closed his eyes.

"I'll make some lunch," Mary called back to him from the kitchen. "Then we'll go and look at those caves!" He remained silent. "Keep you in the shade, eh?"

"Yes," he replied dreamily. "I suppose the weather is rather hotter than usual today..." He felt the plastic handle of the carrier bag cutting into his hands from the weight of the tins and vegetables inside. He wondered how many other holiday-makers had visited in that year alone.

The stunning facade of the house led him to imagine artists and writers alike would be drawn to it. Some of the other cottages in the brochure only showed pictures of the internal rooms, but this one had a double page spread. He remembered looking at it and instantly knowing it was perfect. Four weeks in England would have to rival the French Alps or the Greek islands, it was all they could afford. He admired the ramshackle collection of slanted windows and wooden beams. They had been lovingly preserved, considering how close they were to the sea. He imagined the long succession of owners carefully treating each piece of wood, watching the tar and creosote be eagerly sucked into the dry material. At some point someone had decided to paint the brickwork white, maybe to protect it from the salt-laden wind...

He glanced back to the car in front of the garage. This was clearly a 1930s addition to the building: wooden doors with small panes of glass at the top were also stained black to match the beams of the house. By painting the brickwork and encouraging the roses to climb, the owners had managed to blend the centuries into one.

He watched his wife through the lower kitchen window next to him. She was preparing a picnic lunch. They wanted optimum beach-time; the cool shade of the house could wait until later. The window to the left of the front door framed the tiny living room. Through its polished panes he could see a small sofa and a pine bookcase full of well-thumbed paperbacks. The front door, with its garland of roses, was the original. Its thick dark wood was studded with large iron nails. There was no letterbox or doorbell, just a heavy metal knocker in the shape of a ship. He stared up at the bedroom window and the sun caught his face. Such a warm day, almost too warm... He heard the sound of crockery and cutlery in the kitchen and decided it was his cue to make himself useful. The least he could do was help wash up, and get into more suitable attire for the beach.

*   *   *

A slight breeze wafted across the golden sands, and a shimmering heat haze made the whole beach quiver like a mirage. It was a surprisingly short walk from the cottage, the rest of the village being set back inland, a barrier of fallow fields between them and the sea. Only a couple of fisherman's cottages dared to be so close to the shore. Jon hadn't realised that this particular beach had its own mine situated directly above the caves which opened up at the base of the cliff. He had come across a visitor's guide in the cottage and hungrily scanned the photocopied pages. He wanted to be able to answer any of his wife's questions about the area. He wanted to impress her, still feeling as if the relationship was a ruse and she would one day wake up and leave him for someone more... well... *adventurous*.

The sandy beach was as breath-taking as any foreign holiday resort. The deep blue sea verged on aquamarine as it lapped the shore, without a strand of seaweed in sight. White gulls out over the waves dove down to retrieve their silvery lunchtime treats, surfacing seconds later with their prize. The sand was biscuit-crumb yellow, almost golden; the occasional flash of light reflecting off a glassy grain made the whole stretch sparkle beneath their leather sandals.

As they walked further towards the cliffs Mary skipped ahead. She was carrying the lunch-bag. It swung and bumped around so much that Jon made a mental note to let the lemonade settle for a while when they finally chose their spot. The cliffs were a strange affair. They were not the craggy grey outcrops of Tintagel. The gradual incline towards the mine tricked your mind into believing they were harmless. As they neared the foot of the first section of rocks Mary stared up at them and let a low whistle escape from her lips.
"Wow... they're certainly something..." Jon nodded. Now standing next to them he could see that what had appeared to be grass-covered mud was in fact rough silver granite. Paths of the sparkling stone showed through between the sea pinks and white campion flowers. Scrub grass and fronds of heather seemed to be holding the rock face back, cradling it to the earth.

Suddenly the thought of exploring the damp caves beneath these towering natural buttresses didn't seem so appealing. Beads of sweat were running down his back, collecting in the waistband of his denim shorts... maybe it was the sun playing tricks on him, maybe he *did* need the shade... he wondered how long one could stay outside in this sort of weather before becoming a victim of heatstroke...

After ten more minutes of laboured walking, Mary chose a section of beach just in front of the most formidable cave entrance. It was partially shaded, and being low tide, the sand had already dried to a powder. Solid bulkheads of volcanic rock looked as if they too had melted from the cliff face in the heat, forming piles on the sand that created a small bay. The newly-weds laid out their tartan picnic blanket and Mary began to set out the food: rolls, crisps, cucumber, tomatoes, hard boiled eggs... the sight of this banquet made him feel slightly queasy.

"It looks lovely..." he offered, not wanting to offend her.

"You could sound more enthusiastic!" She laughed. "I'm sure you'll feel better after some food and a nap in the shade." She raised a hand to her forehead to shield her eyes from the sun. "Where do you suppose everyone is?"

John hadn't noticed the lack of people, but it was odd that they were the only patrons of this vast paradise.

"You know what they say: mad dogs and English men..." She punched him playfully.

"And which one am I?" As always Mary was correct. After having eaten the picnic and dozing for half an hour Jon felt revived. He had overcome his anxiety about exploring the cave system, and was actually looking forward to finding the old tin mine machinery. Mary reached into the lunch bag and smiled. She produced his blue leather camera bag.

"Looking for this?" He smiled too, she really was perfect.

"Yes, I thought I left it in the car back at the cottage."

"Don't be silly. It would have melted in this heat. Come on... let's do our best Famous Five impersonation and see what all the mystery is about!" She jumped up, flinging the camera towards him.

The sun had made its way across the sky and was now baking their luncheon spot. Jon caught the camera bag, falling backwards in a cloud of golden dust.

"Hey watch it!" He exclaimed, the sand was so hot he nearly burned his hands as he hoisted himself up. "Last one inside has to pay for drinks later!" Mary and Jon took off their beach clothes to reveal their bathing costumes, leaving their blanket and picnic remains spread across the sand. There was not a soul in sight, not even the hint of a distant fishing boat on the horizon or a rambler on the cliff path above.

They approached the large, dark opening below the long-deserted stone engine house of Wheal Pitts mine. It was pleasant in the gloomy silence of the cave. Ice-cold water dripped from the reddish-green streaked rock with a steady, soothing noise, rather like a grandfather clock. Tick, tick, tick... Jon had brought no torch, so they had to stay within sight of the beach and the opening of the cave. Mary was dipping her toes in a small pool on the edge of the fading light. Any further in and she would have been masked in shadow.

The overwhelming serenity of the sea, which was framed by the inky-black walls of the cave, and the almost musical dripping of the water on the stone played on the sensuous natures of the couple. Forgetting his fear of the darkness he walked over to join Mary at the unlit rock pool, and without speaking they lay down on the dark wet sand to make love. Their passion was heightened by the tantalising, but very slim, chance of discovery. It was as if time was irrelevant; the only thing that existed was their ardour and the shallow cool water surrounding them.

The harsh scream of a passing seabird echoing high above them in the stalactites brought them out of their reverie. The creature swooped into the cavern, demonstrating how truly enormous it was. They both sat transfixed, watching its smooth flight. Against the jet-black of the far wall it could have been an angel... Mary righted herself and continued her exploration of the rock pools, gasping and pointing at the deep red anemones which waved their short tendrils in the current. John was more interested in trying to capture on film the remains of machinery that was used when the cave had been the site of the pump-house engine for the tin mine.

"Did you know there's been a mine on this site since 1692?" He called. Mary made an interested noise. "It's been out of action for almost eighty years."

Jon opened his camera, fitting the small flash bulb so he could take a couple of photographs. He hoped that the light would illuminate the rusted machinery and make for an interesting conversation piece over dinner back home with friends. Mary was chuckling to herself, and when he turned around he saw that she had seductively draped her body over a glistening rock. He smiled. She was ever so beautiful; the sea air and water only enhanced her appealing features. He quickly moved in front of her, with his back to the cave entrance. His aim was to get the perfect shot of her pale body against the shadowy depths of the cave. She let out a peal of laughter and struck a voluptuous pose. Jon pressed the button. The blue-white flash filled the cavern and temporarily blinded her, but instead of approval she heard him cry out in surprise.

Closing her eyes to clear her vision, Mary assumed that the unusual colours in the cave, or the sight of a particularly interesting relic had taken him aback. Her husband reeled forward, confused by what

116

he had just witnessed. Muttering something nonsensical he grabbed Mary's wrist and started hauling her out towards the blistering sunlight. All post-coital lethargy was dissolved in an instant of panic. It was like the last fifteen minutes hadn't even happened. Mary could barely see and was not impressed at being man-handled. She peeled his fingers from her arm and refused to move any further.

"Jon, for God's sake what is it?" She hung back on purpose, forcing him to grab her again and half drag her across the cold sand of the cave, her toes sinking in as they went. "Jesus Jon! What's the matter? Let go – you're hurting me!"

He finally stopped hauling her forward and was able to catch his breath.

"In – In there..." The young man relaxed slightly, bending over, crouching down to try and regain some composure. They had halted at the cave entrance. The sunlit beach and their blanket still seemed a long way off. "Behind you... back there... I saw a man..." He gulped in a breath, "It was a man!" He was panting too hard to speak.

"What!" Mary was almost laughing with embarrassment. Her cheeks flushed red, but she was not one to squirm at an awkward situation. "Is that all? Well, I hope he got his money's worth, then." Jon wasn't amused. "He was probably further in when we arrived and was too flustered to go past us when we..." He stood up.

"No!" His voice echoed around the cave like a gunshot. "This man was a soldier... an old fashioned soldier..." He gesticulated as best he could, struggling to contain his shock. "There was a sword in his hand... *And he was pointing at you!*" Jon seemed rooted to the spot, his eyes flicking back and forth at the blackness behind her.

"Don't be *ridiculous*," Mary said curtly as she led the way out into the blissful sunshine. Jon followed her and immediately felt the atmosphere relax. "Come on, the sun has obviously got to you. Let's go for a proper swim, then I'll make a nice cup of tea back at the cottage. We could eat at the local pub, as a 'first-day' treat."

"Yes..." He replied hesitantly, glancing over his shoulder to what was now just an impenetrable black hole. "Yes, I do need a drink. Besides, the photograph will definitely show I was imagining it. It must have been a trick of the flash." Mary nodded. He kissed the nape of his wife's neck, and then raced her to the sea. "The camera never lies!" He shouted over his shoulder, trying his best to be jovial.

*   *   *

Although the camera's roll of film was only half used, Jon dropped it in at the chemist on the way to the local pub, The Wrecker's Retreat. Mr Edwards wasn't too pleased at the late custom; he'd just totalled up the till, but as his two policies were 'payment in advance' and 'always be polite to tourists', he had to stay behind and sort things out. After all, he was a man of his word.

Jon had decided that he needed the added security of a perfectly normal photograph to allay the fears that 'the cracks' were opening up again. He hoped that those bleak crevices were plastered over for good. Marriage, work and the normality of everyday life had somewhat helped, but in the back of his mind was always the inkling that things could regress. It had been four years since his first fiancée had died in an aircraft collision; three years since the emotional breakdown, the institution, the medication, the awful doctors, specialists and nurses... For the first time in the two

118

years since he'd left the hospital he was worrying about his sanity, and on his honeymoon of all places.

The chemist had promised, between pursed lips that threatened to slide from a smile to a snarl, that he would have the roll of film developed by tomorrow morning. Jon had paid extra up-front for the quick turn- around, and offered his thanks so many times that it had become awkward.

The couple entered the local pub, slightly easier in their minds. Mary was still certain that Jon's mystery man was a self-conscious beach comber, and Jon was almost convinced that he had conjured up this figure from the sudden exposure to the flash in such a wet, reflective area. If he *did* exist, surely he would have seen the man before, when he was photographing the back of the cave before he framed his wife...

The Wrecker's Retreat was an old property of about the same age as the cottage. All the buildings in the village were at least a century old, with the inn, the cottage and the chemist being the most ancient. Oak panelling darkened the bar. Where the wood stopped at shoulder height a smoke stained whitewash continued up and over the peeling ceiling. This was crossed by pocked and blackened oak beams with the occasional horse brass tacked on for good measure. A log fire burned in the grate with no regard to season or outside temperature. The whole place had a well-used, timeless, quality and an impenetrable air of pipe tobacco, even though no one was, at that moment, smoking.

This enduring atmosphere was aided by the landlord, one Moses Creddle. He was the last in line of a local inn-keeping family who had also dabbled in the smuggling trade on the side. Moses had broken with this long-held tradition by joining the British army in 1944 out of choice, before his call-up papers came through. He served mainly in Normandy where some of the 'commodities' that he brought back with him had allowed him to re-enter the family fold as a 'chip off the old block'.

He was eyeing the newly married couple in the bar with bemused interest.

"Knockers Cottage?" He said, with a smile playing around the corners of his mouth. "And you're there the whole month you say? Nice place. Hope you enjoy your stay." He had toyed with the idea of slipping into the 'yokelese' thick Cornish accent he reserved for tourists, but these seemed decent folk. If they were to become regulars he would find the pretence hard to keep up.

As the evening drew on, an excellent meal was washed down with soothing drinks. The mixture of alcohol and sun took its effect. The odd happenings of the day became insignificant; they faded into the general background of 'life experiences'. No more, no less. Jon got into conversation with a group of village men at the bar, matching his somewhat alcoholically embellished ghost story against some of the even taller yarns of the friendly Cornishmen.

The glowing couple left well after closing time, not exactly inebriated, but definitely merry. The night was clear, warm and very still. It was almost tropical in its humidity, with the heat still radiating from the shoreline. Grasshoppers called to each other from the verdant hedgerows, insects buzzed around them in a minuscule symphony. A large summer moon hung over the satin sea, and the ruins of the tin mine buildings above the cave stood silhouetted against the velvet sky. In the moonlight they appeared to be the bones of some long-forgotten prehistoric skeleton.

After a pleasant evening ramble along the winding lane they reached their cottage, Jon unsteadily opened the door, and they turned for a moment to stare at the silvery sea water beyond the cottage garden.

"Listen," Mary attempted a slurred whisper, "I can hear a creaking noise, like wood bending or something..." Jon smothered a chuckle.

"You're drunk Mrs Minton," he whispered back.

"No," she shook his arm. "Shhhh listen." This time he heard the sound as well, like an unoiled gate swinging back and forth in a breeze.

"Just grasshoppers and crickets..." he murmured as they went inside, closing the thick door after them.

Next to the house the old, dead, branches of an ancient oak tree groaned and swayed in an ethereal gale that affected only them.

*   *   *

The sound of the wind awoke Jonathan with a start. It must have risen during the night. The newspaper had mentioned nothing of inclement weather. Normally it would have annoyed him. He found persistent sounds irritating after a while; like a de-tuned radio you can't switch off. However, it would hopefully mean that yesterday's pressing humidity had been swept away. He climbed out of the warm double bed, and ground his fists into his eyes in an attempt to wake up.

His vision still blurred, he opened the bedroom window to let in the fresh morning air. But what he saw from the casement, brought him to full alertness, like a sharp slap on the cheek. The sight that met his astonished gaze was the aftermath of what must have been a great storm. The cottage further up the road had part of its roof ripped off, and tiles littered the lane! Debris of all descriptions adorned the surrounding hedgerows. He looked skyward in amazement, but it became evident that the storm had already blown itself out. A few ragged white clouds raced across a powder-blue background, and the day promised to be a good one. They must have slept heavily to have missed a gale of such magnitude.

Just as he was turning away from the window, he spied a man moving between the trees across the lane at the edge of the opposite field.

"Hello!" Jon called loudly, waking his wife with the sound. The man looked up.

"A good mornin' to you, sir," he hailed back, touching his battered leather cap in an antiquated gesture of respect.

"Big storm last night?" Jon asked from the window, but the man took it as a statement, nodding.

"Aar. Two people had a chimbley fall on 'em, tis said." Jon was glad that he and Mary had slept through what appeared to be a hurricane. The worry about their home in London would only have ruined the honeymoon, possibly even cut it short.

"Do you happen to know what time it is?" He said, suddenly noticing that the radio alarm clock had disappeared from the bedside table behind him. He must have knocked it off in his sleep... Funny how that hadn't woken him up, though... The old man in the field took out a brass pocket watch.

"It be after eight of the clock, master," he replied. Jon rubbed his eyes again. The odd little man was now making his way through the ragged hedge, out into the road. After another few seconds of sleepy contemplation, Jonathan noticed that the 'road' looked as though a heap of stones and earth had been swept over it. He couldn't see an inch of black tarmac anywhere. It must have been hill-wash from the storm, he reasoned with himself.

Come to think of it, it felt like remnants of the lightning's electricity still hung in the air like static. He felt decidedly off-kilter, thankfully the anxiety and edginess of yesterday had gone.

"Seein' as how you're up, sir, I'll prepare the breakfast," said the little old man. He was now in the front garden of the cottage, moving a small fallen branch with the toe of his boot. Jon was taken aback, but assumed that he had missed the 'bed and breakfast' element of the holiday cottage in the catalogue's small-print. The man disappeared round the side of the house, ignoring the front door, past where the brick garage should be. It wasn't.

Jon pulled his torso back in from the cool morning air and closed the window. Maybe the garage was another casualty of the storm? He hoped the horses' carriage was alright... He walked the few steps back to the edge of the bed as if in a daze. *Carriage...?* Where did that word come from? Puzzled, he took his dozing wife's outstretched hand, and looked around at the bedroom. At a quick glance it seemed much the same; the antique furniture and cream linen much as it had been the night before. Yet on closer inspection telling details were different, the missing radio alarm being the most obvious.

"What's wrong?" Mary asked with a yawn. He shook his head.

"Nothing... well... I don't know, it's... strange."

He looked down at the bed. Although the counterpane was formed of the same pale colours as before, it was now changed, displaying examples of exquisite needlework and quilting that would have had a vintage embroidery expert drooling. His nightshirt was also of a heavier material, but again, the same hue as yesterday. All the bedding and nightwear had been included in the rental agreement... Scrutinising the tiny fireplace he saw cold grey ashes where last night there had been a tasteful dried flower arrangement. Mary watched as he tried to take it in. It was all quite bizarre, but somehow it felt strangely familiar.

"So what's happened?" She asked again, climbing out of bed and going over to the wardrobe. "Is someone playing a trick on us? Is this one of those hidden camera shows?"

She felt on top of the wardrobe with her hand, expecting to come into contact with a lens, instead a few balls of dust came floating down. Jon looked around too, trying to reason that there must be a logical explanation for the small changes in the room.

"I don't know," came his reply, "but we'd better get dressed and find out." The clothes that they discovered in the wardrobe were certainly not the seventies' latest fashion, in fact it seemed that all of their own T-shirts and jeans had been replaced with replica clothes from a bygone era. As the couple dressed in stunned silence, the eighteenth century fastenings and buttons presented little difficulty to their fingers.

Mary somehow knew how to adjust the undergarments and in what order to tie the bows on the side of her skirts. Everything seemed to fit. For a brief instant Jonathan thought his wife looked like she was trying on a replica fancy dress costume in a museum. A brief image of the sanitised, austere hospital flashed into his mind unbidden, and for just an instant he was totally overcome. He saw the beds around him, noted the defibrillators against the wall, the visitors of other patients, he belonged in that world – no! He didn't! He was here with Mary, he was happy... wasn't he?

Shaking his head to remove the unwanted memory, he looked around the quaint room. There was definitely something wrong, someone had to be playing a prank on them. Maybe their friends had set it up as a honeymoon trick. The stag night had been uneventful, this could be pay back. He scanned the room again. This was absurd. Clothes and furniture didn't change overnight, they weren't so drunk that they passed out from the hoppy ale; they would have heard people entering the cottage. He touched the windowsill and felt the white painted wood firm beneath his hands. At least the cottage was real.

...Or was it? The fog came down over his senses again. He had only a hazy awareness of his own present reality. Worryingly – if he could remember why he should be worried – he felt increasingly calm about accepting this new situation. His wife's placid expression told him that she was feeling the sensation too.

*   *   *

The stretch of sandy beach was all but deserted, barely recognisable from the calm oasis of the previous day. The impressive cliffs followed slightly different contours, as though some of the rock falls seen yesterday near the cave had not yet occurred yet. But when *was* yesterday? There was a realisation in the back of each of their consciousnesses that the impossible had, quite possibly, happened. They held hands with a vice-like grip, trying to remain grounded.

Breakfast had been a strange affair of thick cut toast made from home made bread (which neither of them remembered buying from the supermarket). The man at the porcelain sink seemed to be a blur, boiling a large black kettle on a fire in the kitchen grate that materialised from nowhere. He gave them butter in a mottled ceramic pot, and the cutlery seemed misshapen in a way that Jon had not noticed before. He desperately clutched at straws, praying that it was just the fact he had been so preoccupied with his sunstroke and the long drive down. He couldn't have been paying attention when Mary prepared the picnic.

Once the old man left the kitchen to "attend to moi other work", the confused couple decided to take a stroll to the beach. When they left the cottage Jon realised that he was missing something crucial. He looked to the left of the building and blinked. A thin stone path snaked its way close to the house and around to the back kitchen door... just as it always had... There was no cause for alarm. The scrubby patch of grass that formed the front garden was covered in twigs and leaves from the unexpected summer storm. Only the thick, twisted oak tree seemed undamaged. It was swaying slightly. Jon found it hard to focus on the highest limbs. He blamed the bright sky above.

All the way to the beach there had been signs of the gale. The local people, dressed in the same strange attire as the couple, seemed mainly worried that the tin mine hadn't flooded. There were certainly more people around than yesterday: children and parents combing the shoreline, young men with dogs shouting to each other with urgent voices. No one gave the newly-weds a second glance, unless it was to wish them a good morning and a "how have you fared", in an overly familiar way.

The accents were much thicker than Jon and Mary were used to; even the men in the pub last night had been easily understood, but *these* folk... Mary stared around her, still mute with either trepidation, or amusement – Jon couldn't tell which. Curiously he felt like they were part of a large scale television costume drama, or a game show where the rules of winning were unclear. Perhaps they had to survive a day in the life of a... Mary was clasping his hand rather more tightly than when they had walked down the thin muddy lane. Now on the open beach she seemed overwhelmed. On the flat, wreckage-strewn, sands she

126

suddenly burst into tears. A few passers-by looked up and changed their course to avoid the sobbing mistress.

"I don't like it Jon!" She wailed. "If this is some kind of damned local joke to get rid of us, then it's not in very good taste! And if your mates from work have paid for this charade then it's a waste of bloody money!" He tried to console her, but found himself growing agitated. It wasn't so bad: the storm was over. They could get back to running the farm in just a few hours...

"My dearest Mary, whatever can be wrong?" He asked, the words flowed from his mouth while his eyes were transfixed on the bizarre scene. "This all seems quite right my love. The storm was wild, yet we are unharmed. It... it doesn't scare me like it should."

Mary shook free of his hand and pulled her shawl tighter around her shoulders. Rays from the morning sun caught the calm water of the sea and made it sparkle like shattered glass. The wreckage on the beach consisted almost entirely of wood, some of it painted. Jon felt bad for any sailors caught close to the rocky shore when the worst of the weather hit the coast. Great piles of seaweed lay heaped against the bottom of the cliffs. Already some enterprising people were piling the slimy black fronds onto barrows and carts to use as fertiliser. Nothing of nature's bounty was being wasted. He mused on the scene for a few moments; something was pricking the back of his mind.

Of plastic bottles, tyres, black oil, and nylon rope there was no sign. No discarded orange polythene cord in the flotsam and jetsam. No broken remnants of buoys. A part of him deep down asked 'what is plastic?' He shuddered. The part of him that remembered could only say; 'you have to remember that plastic is real, all of this historical nonsense isn't.' He looked at the weeping figure of his new wife, then across to some of the local men who had stopped searching the beach and were smoking stubby clay pipes at the bottom of the rugged cliff path. He looked at the empty blue sky and somehow he knew without a doubt that they'd stepped back in time.

He felt like a new boy at a school dance. How was one supposed to behave? What were the rules about disturbing your own time-line by new actions in the past? How did one get back to the correct era? Rather incongruously he wished he'd read more science fiction. He had eagerly consumed HG Wells' 'The Time Machine', but that dealt with travelling to the future. He tried to recall any scientific radio programmes he had heard over the years; how he wished he'd chosen Radio Four over the popular music stations. Song lyrics buzzed around his head, and he tried to think clearly. The past was something he should know about; he'd studied history and geography at school for several years. What he wanted more than anything else at this precise moment was to be sitting at his dining table in London listening to the Breakfast Show on the wireless with a nice cup of tea and some biscuits...

While he was contemplating their situation Mary had discovered something among the wood on the beach that confirmed his fears. With remarkable composure, considering the state she had just been in, she was crouching by an object. It was difficult to identify because it was tangled with a large amount of green seaweed. Her mind seemed to have become fuzzy again, and she was cruising on some kind of instinct, acting almost as an automaton. She pulled some of the sodden weed away and stood up. Jon was able to identify the corpse of a naval officer dressed in a tattered blue coat.

"This is a real body," said Mary monotonously. No sense of shock or fear. "A real body... In real clothes, on a real beach, after a real storm." Jon nodded and looked around them.

"I think so... Yes. All these other people are real, as well," he replied. With an effort, he tried to focus. "We mustn't let anyone suspect a thing – just say we're really tired from the storm last night, or something..." Mary turned to face him. She was pale, he felt helpless. "We should listen as much as possible, and talk as little as politeness will allow. It's the only way to keep up this pretence." Mary's lip began to wobble again.

"I promise I'll try, but my head feels so hazy, like my brain is stuffed with cotton wool. A migraine perhaps... I can't think straight..." Over her shoulder, he caught sight of the short, wiry, man who had cooked them breakfast He was hurrying towards them, rather like a human crab, bent over almost into a crouch.

"Good day, Sir. I wish to thank you for a most enjoyable breakfast," Jon said, uncertain of how he was supposed to speak, or indeed whom he was supposed to speak to. The little man seemed to find this highly amusing, and guffawed loudly, wiping his eyes with a cream coloured kerchief.

"Sir? Sir? Ee, master, you will have your jokes. Here oi be, old Jess Creddle, served your family nigh on thirty year, and you be calling *me* 'sir'. That be a good'un, that be." At least that saved the bother of introductions, but what were they to do now? There was an embarrassed silence which Jonathan eventually broke.

"Well, then, Jess. Will you not join my wife and I in a spot of something warming in the Wrecker's Retreat?"

Second mistake. He wanted to usher the words back into his mouth but it was impossible. Women of Mary's class did not enter inns or taverns. Luckily this was lost to the third mistake he'd made, which was more relevant to Creddle at any rate.

"I'd be roight glad to, a bit later sir, but the only inn round here be the Pit Tavern, as well you knows, Mr Minton. Ain't never heard of no *Wrecker's Retreat* in these parts, oi'm sure." Mary attempted to save the situation with a quick glance at Jon.

"Please excuse my husband," she began. "He bumped his head last night trying to secure the windows, and neither of us had much sleep. Our brains are slightly addled." The old man nodded solemnly.

"Yours, and many others, I've no doubt, ma'am." Mr Creddle then took his leave with a "well, must be off, things to be a doing of." Something suddenly registered with Jon and his blood ran cold.

"*He said my name.*" He whispered to Mary. She frowned, unsure of the importance.

"Well, it *is* your name – Mr Minton." She whispered back.

"But how did *he* know? I haven't told him. If you pinch me very hard, will I wake up in the hospital? Will this be some medication-fuelled delusion..." She looked at him quizzically. Her eyes misted over and a smile played around her lips.

"What hospital would that be my dearest?" He closed his eyes. It wasn't a dream, and Mary was beginning to lose her fragile hold on reality.

*   *   *

"Hey, George!" The chemist's disembodied voice emanated from the darkroom at the back of the pharmacy. The assistant left the front counter and met his employer by the till. The shop was so small that this required only one step from each of them. The chemist handed over a flimsy packet of photographs. "Can you take these over to the Wrecker's? Chap wanted them done quickly, but hasn't been in here today. He's already paid. Only used about a third of the film. Happen Moses will see him before the day's out."

George took the prints, and with no thought to the customer's privacy, glanced at them one by one.

"Odd lot of photos," he mused, selecting one at random. "Half of 'em haven't been exposed. Must be some historical society using the beach at the moment... Look at this soldier in the cave behind the bird in the tight bikini... Looks like a bloody corpse. Bunch of weird folk if you ask me, should let battles be bygones." He replaced the prints in their paper sheath.

"Hmmm," muttered the chemist, who had barely glanced at them when he was carrying out the developing.

"I did notice *that* one, actually. I mean, who wouldn't? Oh, well, if he don't come back for them, Moses can stick 'em up in the bar to add a bit of colour." George chuckled at his employer's idea, and then made his way leisurely over to the pub.

*   *   *

Mary had eventually left her husband at the tavern (with it's former name), in what she hoped were the safe hands of Jess Creddle. It was obviously no place for the wife of a yeoman farmer, so she ambled back to the cottage in a daze and tried to pull her muddled thoughts together. Her emotions slid from despair (whenever she tried to address her predicament), to peaceful acquiescence of the situation.

She wasn't afraid, and in some respects that was what worried her. Jon had a nervous disposition on occasion, and she always pulled him through. Now she was quickly realising that neither she, nor her husband held the solution as to how to return themselves to their own time... if indeed that was what they had to do. She stood quietly for a moment in the front garden of the cottage.

Local children had been picking up sticks and branches for their families' wood stores. The fresh green grass was almost immaculate. She looked at the front door with its wooden arbour. There were no pink roses adorning it, she tried to recall what the cottage had looked like yesterday. Roses, white painted window frames, a garage for their... what was it again? An *automobile*... a carriage... she shook her head. Never a great church goer, she wondered if this was some kind of divine punishment for something they had done in the past, but she quelled that with a brisk word with herself. 'Oh, don't be so ridiculously old fashioned.' She tried not to laugh at the irony of the thought, but it was pointless. She let out a giggle, and then a chuckle, soon she was doubled over, trying to catch her breath between bouts of hysterics.

A couple of older local women walked past pushing small barrows full to the brim with seaweed. They stared at her, tutting and muttering through their teeth about "indecent behaviour"...She didn't care. This was unbelievable, a farce. *Old fashioned!* She was centuries before her time!

After more cramp-inducing bursts of mirth she righted herself, wandering a while around the garden. As she passed the large oak tree a breeze whispered past her cheek. It was icy cold and she shuddered. The shade cast from its outstretched – almost pleading – branches was chilling, yet the midday sun was pleasantly warm. She looked up through the mass of green leaves and budding acorns. It seemed ever so high, much higher than the thirty or so feet it really was. As she peered into the swaying upper branches she began to feel dizzy. She decided to spend the rest of the day in bed, hiding from the strange, unfamiliar world.

132

Her husband arrived back late in the evening, slightly intoxicated. To her frantic questioning, he could only reply that somehow he was apparently involved in a smuggling caper, and that on the morrow he had to go with Jess Creddle to watch for a ship from the cliff top. Mary felt both alarmed and serene at the same time. This information seemed *natural*. He would be following the procedure for the smuggling run just as he always did... the nagging thoughts of danger pricked at her conscience. Danger from what? Danger from the coast guard who would come and arrest him in their patrol cars? Danger from having a criminal record blemishing their good family name? What was the worry?

As they climbed into bed Jon started to speak about a meeting and a plan, but he was vague and listless. His focus flitted from her face, to the window, to the bedroom door. Mary decided that she too would go to the cliffs with him. One of them had to try and remember. One of them had to remain in...well...the future. Jon kissed her goodnight and made himself comfortable; as comfortable as could be expected, in his long night gown. Mary did the same, the excess material wrapping around her legs like swaddling. She fervently hoped tomorrow would find them both back firmly in the latter years of the twentieth century. Whereas Jon sank quickly into a deep sleep, his wife tossed and turned restlessly into the early hours of the morning. She drifted in and out of dreams; memories plagued her, both real and imagined. She cried.

*　　　*　　　*

The next day dawned sunny and cloudless, as was the norm for Cornwall at that time of year (whatever year it happened to be). The most southerly point in England had the advantage of fine weather and an almost Mediterranean climate. The Cornish peninsula had long been the holiday destination of choice for anyone who dreaded the guaranteed hassle of foreign travel, but desired a deep bronze tan and sandy beaches.

Jon dared not open his eyes. If he did and he saw that the radio alarm clock was still not on the bedside table he was sure he would expire then and there from stress. Mary moved next to him and made some complaint about her night clothes being too hot. He turned onto his side and felt the cloth bunch up around him. Without even looking he knew the radio would not have been replaced.

After a quiet, sobering, breakfast of luke-warm porridge and water, the couple decided that whatever happened they would stick to their rule of not making themselves conspicuous. Jon was nursing a mild hangover and cursed the fact that he had been foolish enough to suggest a drink the day before.

"I just don't know why I went there..." He said dolefully, prodding at the lumpy oatmeal with his spoon. "I felt like I owed Jess something, I can't explain it, I knew we had decided to lay low and just listen politely but I..." He trailed off and Mary laid her hand on his.

"You don't need to tell me. The whole village probably thinks I'm a lunatic after my hysterics in the garden. If I'd been at the pub with you I'd have been legless no doubt... Oh, this is all so tiring!" She was about to tell Jon of the strange sensation she had felt by the oak tree when Jess Creddle entered the kitchen via the back door.

"Ah!" said the little man, touching his forelock, "Mr Minton, oi were held up by the farrier, one of the 'orses lost a shoe yesterday. Awful sorry oi missed breakfast." Jon looked at Mary apologetically.

"That's quite alright. I'm glad to see you. Now, about this business we -" Jess cut him off and motioned for him to stay quiet.

"Not now sir, there's all kinds of people knockin' about this morning. Save it for the cliffs, eh." Mary stared hot pokers at Jon, willing him to excuse himself from whatever he had got himself into. He smiled thinly.

"Very well, the cliff top it is. I shall just get into my boots and we can leave forthwith." He savoured the words as they left his lips. It sounded... correct. Jess didn't bat an eyelid. He checked his battered brass pocket watch.

"Oi'll be seeing you up by the mine shortly." With a nod to Mary he scuttled out of the kitchen and Jon relaxed.

"I'm sorry my love! I didn't know what to do!" He said, his voice cracking slightly. "I was sort of hoping this was all a dream, but waking up here again... What if this is it? What if we're never going back." Mary sighed.

"You're his employer, he would have done whatever you said! You could have cancelled the arrangement!"

"And what about the other men at the tavern? We talked for hours. I agreed to – I don't even *know* what I agreed to – but if I backed out I'm sure it would have looked bad for us." He pushed the heavy ceramic bowls away across the table, they almost tumbled onto the floor. "There has to be a way out of this; not just the business with Jess, this whole era. Maybe if we..." He tapped his fingers on the table top. "We could try and get back to London. What if it's just this village, Cornwall... if we crossed the county line..." He saw that Mary had that far-away look in her eyes again and decided not to press the matter. "I'll only be gone for an hour or so. I promise I won't agree to anything else, anything illegal."

*   *   *

Moses Creddle entered the pharmacy clutching the packet of unclaimed photographs. The only person in there was the young assistant, arranging a delivery of toiletries on the appropriate shelves.

"Mornin' George, another nice day," he offered. The young man leaped backwards and banged his elbow on the glass topped counter.

"Bloody hell… Moses, you didn't half give me a scare. What can I do for you?"

"I came about those photos you brought over yesterday." The innkeeper slapped the packet down on the counter. "Those people didn't come back, and there's no point putting these up in the bar, our customers don't really go for that sort of thing. That one of the young lady in the cave is far too… 'up front' if you get my meaning."

George took the paper pack of photographs.

"Yeah, but I bet your regulars wouldn't complain." Moses agreed with a nod.

"Dare say; dare say, but their bloody wives will!" The men laughed. "No moi lad, I need somethin' with local *historical interest* for the village notice board."

"But -" George grabbed at the prints and rapidly thumbed through them. "There were people in old fashioned clothes on the beach shots. I saw them myself. Long dresses, military gear and such – a man in uniform in the cave too, where have they gone?" He flicked through every photo, and just as Moses had

136

said, the only people in the photographs were Mary and Jonathan Minton.

"P'raps they'm on tea break," said Moses Creddle in an attempt at humour, then a thought crossed his mind. "Are you 'undred percent sure the photos are different from when you handed 'em over t'me?" George nodded.

"Yeah; the same photos from yesterday I'm positive, but the pictures have changed a bit." There was a quiet moment where Moses scratched his stubbled chin.

"Knocker's Cottage." The words meant nothing to George, but Moses continued thoughtfully. "That'll be near two hundred year ago this month... not again, surely can it be..." George, having London origins treated this display of over-dramatic foreboding with a pinch of metropolitan salt – though the thing with the photographs had unnerved him a bit.

"Not *what* again?" He asked, feeling a predictable answer was in the offing, Moses looked around the empty shop and lowered his voice.

"That cottage I tell you... The one they rent out by the beach," he sucked a deep breath in conspiratorially. "They say it's... evil." George had to smother a smile.

"I know the amount they charge for holidays is pretty steep, but..." Moses reached out and earnestly grabbed his wrist.

"Cursed, boy! Why do you think no one 'as lived in it for any length of time?"

George hadn't really given it much thought, he'd only moved to the village for a change of pace and a healthy interest in the leisurely summer beach-life. "Why do you think the present owners don't live there? Why do they stay away!" Moses pressed.

"Probably 'cause they're making more money by renting it out." George was getting irritated by the landlord's tall tale. He started to place bottles of nail varnish remover on the shelf again. "Blimey; evil you say? Who'd have thought it. Nobody says stuff like that anymore." He chuckled as he unwrapped another carton of plastic bottles. "No wonder they think you're all backward bumpkins down here." Moses stepped away from him, taking offence.

"You don't know our ways lad! You've not been 'ere long enough yet. Reckon a few more moons in the village an' you'll feel the same as us." George tried to politely ignore him. "Smugglers, brewers, farmers and the like – our families go back centuries. There's stories that gets told that you never forget." The young man thought this statement too corny for words. He finished stacking the bottles, and went to move on to the next box. He found Moses' dirty work boot resting on the closed lid. "Oi *know* you saw those photos, an' you *know* what was on 'em." George pushed Moses' foot off the box and continued to check the dispatch note against the contents. "You should listen to what 'appened all them years ago... If you don't believe me afterwards, then oi'll leave."

George put down the piece of paper and folded his arms in resignation. After all it was better than working, and there *were* the odd photos to think about... still, it was a tale more suited to a winter's evening in the dark tavern bar, than a hot summer's day in an empty village pharmacy.

"Well," Moses leaned forward conspiringly. "Just over two hundred years ago, a young gentleman, a farmer 'e was, lived at Knockers Cottage with his new wife, a beautiful young woman who he'd met in Bath..." George rolled his eyes.

"You should have written a romantic book," he found himself interrupting, but in truth it was to try and lighten the suddenly heavy atmosphere. The shop seemed much smaller than it had a minute ago. Moses frowned.

"It was known locally that the farm was not doing very well due to fallin' prices for selling livestock and such. But the young man seemed comfortable enough. The assumption was that 'e was mixed up with the free traders." George's face was blank. It was Moses turn to roll his eyes. "Think lad, think! Them's the *smugglers*. Well, the local Revenue Officer took a fancy to the farmer's pretty new wife, and did all in his power to catch the farmer at his night work. The man didn't hide his infatuation, and there was 'ventually a set-to between the officer and the farmer." Moses waited for a passer-by to move on from the shop window before he continued.

"Well, not long afterwards t'was a bad storm, and they found the body of the Revenue Officer on the beach below the cliff... with his neck broken, see. Folk didn't know if it were an accident or something else. Soon afterwards the farmer and his wife disappeared; most people say they went back to Bath... They certainly weren't seen round 'ere again." For an instant everything pressed in, and it was difficult to breathe in the crowded room full of packed shelves and medicine bottles, then there was an almost audible 'pop'.

It was like coming out of a railway tunnel at high speed. The atmosphere cleared in a moment. The two men were facing each other, neither one of them wanting to acknowledge what had just happened. George cleared his throat.

"That's... pretty old hat, Moses. I assume that the young farmer bloke was supposed to have killed the Revenue Officer, then fled with his wife... typical! And I suppose that now the cottage is *haunted*." He scoffed at the idea, gaining back some of his bravado. Moses was almost losing his composure.

"Yes lad! Yes! And oi fear that those 'oliday makers are in danger. This ain't no joking matter, there's things here that are not to be meddled with."

"I thought you'd say something like that. How do you know all this guff, anyway?" George asked as he glanced once more at the pile of photos on the counter.
"The person who lived in the cottage after they'd gone was my," he began to count on his fingers. "Great-great-great-grandfather's brother. 'E had been a servant to the farmer an' his family, always said as how 'e didn't think they had gone back to Bath... Never told anyone what really happened, and took his opinions to the grave." George glanced at the clock. Its ticking had become an irritation.

"Look, I'm closing for lunch now, I've got half an hour. How about coming over to that cottage with me? I can give the people the photos, and you can tell them your history of the place... they'll probably lap it up. I bet the owners won't thank you for it, though." Moses shuddered at the thought.
"Oi've a feeling that we're already too late. There won't be no one there now..."
"Oh *come on*," sighed George, removing his white coat, and trying to sound more skeptical than he felt, "I've always wanted to see a ghost."

*   *   *

The wind was only slightly diminished, and the persistent tones of Jess Creddle gave the impression that even death would not silence them. When the little old man and Jonathan set out for the cliff, Mary, without her husband's knowledge, followed at a discreet distance. She had concluded that the only possible way of escape from this nightmare was to stay close to Jon at all times. This she intended to do, even if he forbade it. Without drawing attention to herself, she used the low bushy undergrowth and stunted trees as barriers between them. The cliff top path was narrow and laced with hard lumps of stone. Through the foliage she could see everything, but remained shielded from view.

High on the cliff, several yards below the well-trodden track, Jess Creddle and Jon lay flat on their stomachs on the close, rabbit cropped turf. They were gazing out to sea, shielding their eyes against the summer sun. Below them, and a long way off, a tiny white dot stood out against the undulating blue water. Despite the stiff breeze that continued over the land, the ocean was relatively calm. Jess handed a brass telescope to the younger man, and they both stared at the sail as it zig-zagged towards the shore on an uncertain course. Jon mused that he could very easily get used to this kind of existence... the company was good, the clothes were rough yet serviceable; he'd never been a great fan of the television... but he was worried about his wife. It would not do to let her know that he was warming to the simple existence, and he was aware that he knew nothing about farming, which was his supposed profession...

"As we arranged, she'm goin' to stand off until ten of the clock tonight," the old man was whispering hoarsely. The words didn't reach Mary in her hiding place. "We figured as how it was still too early in the day for the Revenue to be properly prepared." Jon nodded.

"And... where do we hide the cargo this time?" He asked gingerly.

"Tunnels below the mine, same as always." Jess motioned to the area above the caves at the bottom of the cliff. Jon remembered how deep and dank they had been. A perfect place for contraband.

One of the main things that was plaguing Mary was that the wind was blowing the words away from her. Exasperated, she had crept closer to them, but that also meant leaving the security of her hide, and being uncomfortably close to the edge of the cliff. There was a slight dip where she could crouch down. If they happened to look back she could pretend she was fastening her shoe and had come looking for Jon for some errand or another.

The pair were talking in such low voices. She felt she couldn't let them out of her sight, so she resigned herself to spending much of the morning laying flat-out in the longer grass by the warm rock of the bluff. It wasn't too uncomfortable. Despite herself, she drifted off into a nap while studying the light pink flowers and small grey lichens that were next to her elbows.

"Watching for coneys, my pretty?" The coarse voice suddenly coming out of nowhere, made her heart skip a beat. She gasped involuntarily, nearly rolling to the edge of the rock. She found herself staring into the most vile face she had ever seen. Dressed in a blue uniform, with grubby breeches that had once been white, the man's hand rested on the hilt of a regulation government issue sword which he wore on a strap slung over his right shoulder.

His face was a mass of tiny purple scars from acne, or was it smallpox? Thin crimson lips cut across his chin like another scar. Above this a pitted nose, discoloured by years of drinking, protruded between two malicious, rat-like eyes. She blinked a few times to try and clear her sleepy vision. He spoke again.

"Waiting for coneys, *my pretty*? Or are you waiting for some swain to come along? A secret cliff top tryst, eh?" Not knowing that coneys were rabbits, and mistaking the word 'swain' for 'swine' due to the man's accent, Mary bridled.

"I'm quite alright, thank you," came her haughty reply. She carefully stood up, minding not to step on the hem of her long skirts.

Without a backward glance she started to walk off briskly back to the uneven main path. She was just about to make her way down the track towards the tin mine and her husband, when a rough hand clamped down onto her shoulder.

"Not so fast, my dear." The throaty, malingering voice came again. She stopped walking.

"I'll thank you to *take your hand off me*," she hissed through gritted teeth.

"Now then, my pretty, you surely wouldn't begrudge a poor old soldier a kiss..."

Mary was appalled, and wondered if her husband had seen them.

"Look," she cried, panic and loathing welling up inside her. "Leave me alone or I'll have the law onto you!" The man took his hand off her and started to sneer.

"*Law*?" he mocked, swathing her in a tight stinking, embrace, "Hah! Law? I *am* the law, as well you know!" He thrust his twisted face close to hers; his breath was even worse than his body odour. Personal hygiene was obviously foreign to him. Mary screamed, and at the same time brought her knee up sharply to his groin, but the cumbersome skirt slowed the movement and all impetus was lost. This made him even more determined to gain his prize. One of the coarse, swollen, hands fumbled with the back of her clothes and she screamed with all her might.

*　　*　　*

The beautiful cottage seemed to be deserted, several wasted minutes spent banging on doors and windows appeared to confirm this.

"The car's still here; they can't have gone far," observed George, peering through one of the windows of the vehicle and spying a road map on the back seat.

"They're tourists lad. They could've walked ten miles away by now," said Moses despondently. The chemist's assistant relaxed.

"Well then, what are we worried about? They've probably gone for a hike. Perhaps they've decided to camp away for a couple of days... people do that you know."

Moses Creddle was not really listening. His eyes focussed in disbelief on the old oak tree next the cottage. George followed his gaze.

"Look! Look at that! It ain't natural." The young man glanced up, and gasped with astonishment. Sultry as the day was, the old gnarled branches were clacking and knocking together, as though tossed by a winter's gale. George grabbed the old man's arm, and pulled him back from the garden into the lane, away from the cottage. As he did so, the windows seemed – just for an instant – to distort, like the surface of a trampoline when weight is applied... Once in the road, on the hard tarmac, everything seemed normal. George saw a discarded beer can and an empty packet of cigarettes in the grass of the verge. The oak tree was still, and the lower window panes reflected the steady images of two startled men.

"W-what do we do now?" Stumbled George, a knot of excitement tightening in his stomach. He was getting his wish regarding an eventful summer.

"We must get into that house no matter what. Better get the police though, can't be gettin' accused of breakin' and enterin'. Oi'll get me public licence taken away." They headed to the Wrecker's Retreat to use the phone, and to both partake of a stiff drink.

*   *   *

The two men conspiring on the cliff top swung round at the sound of a woman's scream.

"That's my wife!" Cried Jonathan, leaping up, and breaking into a run.

"Hell's bells! That's Captain Millgard, the Riding Officer!" called Jess, jogging after him as fast as his old legs could manage. "Be careful, master, he's always armed!" Out of the corner of his lecherous eyes the Captain caught sight of the two figures running towards him. He flung Mary to one side as though she were nothing but a bale of hay. She scrambled away from the cliff edge, trying desperately to straighten her clothes.

Captain Millgard drew a rusty, badly maintained, pistol from his belt. A puff of smoke and the dangerous lead ball flew harmlessly past Jon's legs. Before the officer could draw his sword, the inflamed husband was upon him, and they were rolling in the coarse grass at the edge of the precipice. Jon brought the filthy writhing man to a halt with a well-timed sharp knee to his bulging stomach, then hauled the massive frame to its feet again. Their eyes met in a confrontation of pure hatred.

"So the little smuggler wants to fight, does he?" The Captain spat with derision.

"You bastard!" Mary heard her husband shout. He swung his arm round, and grabbed at the Captains empty pistol, just as three brightly attired soldiers appeared by the tin mine further along the cliff. Neither of the fighters could see them, but Mary called out to

145

stop Jon handling the weapon, and then she fell back in amazement -

...Everything around her began to happen in slow motion, the edges of her vision smudged, blurred like an out of focus photograph.

The soldiers started running, as Jon's fist smashed square onto the officer's jaw. The big man, unable to balance his overweight body, toppled backwards slowly, oh so slowly, out and over the cliff edge. A final, cursing, scream resounded like a gong,
"I'll see you in Hell!"

Then everything went black.

*   *   *

The police constable was very dubious about breaking into the pristine, unassuming cottage. He would have dismissed Moses' story as an old man's ramblings but for the fact that George was so agitated. Constable Geddes stood before the cottage door and wished that his sergeant was there too.
"You take a look son," Sergeant Brady had said. "I'm sure you can manage, it's only a house call." Now 'managing' seemed to be the last thing that he could do.
        As soon as he had laid a hand on the front door, something flung him back onto the road with a kick like a mule. It was like grabbing the line of an electric fence and feeling your shoulder wrench out of its socket. From the lane he could see the branches of the old oak tree clacking away in their own mysterious wind. He cleared his throat. Moses' tall tale suddenly gained even more credibility.

"Now what do we do?" Geddes helplessly asked the older man.

"I don't know..." Moses was getting anxious. He disliked the police at the best of times; trust issues left over from his family's past. "You're the policeman. Smash a window or somethin'." The same repelling force surrounded the casements, and Geddes found himself in the road once again.

This time he was lying on his back in a very undignified manner. His temper began to boil. In any other situation it would have been comical, but in the eerily empty lane with only two scared men for company he was fuming.

"Now come on," he muttered to himself. "Someone is playing a game here, and I don't think it's very funny..." A headline flashed into his mind; 'P.C. Smashes Cornish Drugs Ring. Awarded Promotion'. That would be a nice coup for the station. Reality intervened in the form of George and some pebbles he had collected from the edge of the field behind them.

Geddes balanced a sizeable rock in his hand and launched it at one of the ground floor windows. Then he threw himself to the ground, as it whizzed back with double the force, embedding itself in the verge across the road, almost five inches deep.

"What the bloody hell is going on?!" cried the exasperated constable, throwing another smaller stone at the house. This time, by chance, the other-worldly force deflected it in the wrong direction. It bounced off the oak tree and then back towards the cottage. A small hole appeared in the bottom of the kitchen window pane.

Moses' cheer was silenced by the deafening and immediate action of the casement: in one swift action glass and wooden frame exploded outwards, scattering splinters over a wide area of the front garden.

A few shards landed as far as the lane and the men jumped back in shock.

"*Did you see that?!* What on earth is in that cottage?!" shouted George, losing his temper and, frustratedly siding with Constable Geddes.

"I... I don't know, lad," replied Moses fearfully. "But we've got to get to the bottom of this once and for all."

*   *   *

Slowly she opened her eyes. Blue; all she could see was blue. What had happened? The wind had dropped, and she felt the hot summer sun on her body; then why... a seagull swooped across the blue on a thermal, and she realised that it was the sky. That was the sky; she was the woman; the woman was on the ground... and the woman was only wearing a long white nightdress and leather bedroom moccasin slippers. Jonathan. Jon... her husband!

The thought erupted in her brain, spreading its lava of fear and worry into the far recesses of her mind. She leapt to her feet, discovered that she was dizzy, and standing on the well-used cliff path somewhere near the village. Instinct told her two things: that she was definitely back in the twentieth century, and that she had to get back to the cottage as quickly as possible. The problem was that, when she shielded her eyes to look for a familiar landmark, she couldn't even see the crumbling carapace of the tin mine or the pump house. She knew that if she was to walk back in the direction of the holiday cottage she needed to keep the sea to her left, so she started her shaking journey on unsteady feet, praying that she would meet someone along the way.

*   *   *

Inside the cottage bedroom, Jonathan Minton sat on the floor, marvelling at his strange apparel. His first thoughts were of his wife; where was she? His second thoughts were of the guttural animal cry that still rang in his ears. His head ached, and he could remember nothing... Nothing except taking his film to the chemist and then drinking too much at the local pub. Walking back with Mary, watching the sea in the moonlight...

He stood up slowly and peered out of the window. The oak tree was still waving and swaying in the heat of the summer's day. His car was parked on the short gravel drive in front of the dilapidated closed doors of the garage. He felt inside the capacious pockets of his alien clothes for some clue as to where he'd been or what had happened. He wondered if there had been a competition at the pub that he had forgotten... maybe an evening summer fete... The pockets were empty, save for a battered leather tobacco pouch and a broken clay pipe. He didn't even smoke. He scratched his chin. A day's worth of stubble. "Mary..." he called weakly through chapped lips. "Where are you? What's going on?"

*   *   *

"Listen," said Moses, moving as close as he dared to the dark void which was now the empty kitchen window casement. "Oi... thought oi heard a voice..." A door crashed against an internal wall upstairs, and the sound of shouting came as if from a long way off. The

149

shouting sounded angry. No one outside dared to move any nearer the opening. Geddes wondered if he would get his fabled 'drugs' bust' after all, the man sounded crazy, maybe he was high as a kite. The day might have been bright, but the house was as inviting as a tomb.

*   *   *

"Excuse me, please, officer, can you help me...?" The sergeant leaned out of his patrol car and took in the sight before him. The woman was obviously upset. She hadn't a clue as to where she was. And, to judge from the mud spattered, soaking, nightdress that was clinging to the point of indecency, she was obviously unhinged. She was looking around her, confused and anxious.

"Why don't you get in the car, miss. I can give you a lift home." Mary appreciatively climbed into the back and told him the address of the cottage. "Ah, that's over in the next cove, just a few miles." The vehicle roared off, she was grateful to hear the familiar noise of a diesel engine, so grateful that she started to sob.

*   *   *

The man who stood blocking the bedroom doorway was dressed in bedraggled uniform of a Naval Captain and apart from being grossly overweight he looked as though someone had recently attempted to push his face through a brick wall. The uniform was tattered and filthy; a horrible smell of wet decay hung around it. Jon was too angry to be frightened, he addressed himself to the disgusting creature in a loud, confident voice.

"Who the hell are you! Get out of this cottage immediately!"

"Min...ton," the throaty voice chilled him to the marrow, "I said I'd see you in hell... Two hundred years I've waited, and now the time is right for me to fulfil that promise. It is now that we duel..."

The bloated 'thing' lunged forward, dripping a slick vile secretion onto the polished floorboards.

"W-who are you?" asked Jon, trying to avoid the malicious gaze of the creature's two beady eyes. "How do you know my name?" The foul beast sputtered a disgusting peal of laughter through his ragged lips.

"Don't try to hold me up, Minton! I always keep my promises. I've had two hundred years to plan this moment... it's just a shame that young Mary isn't here to see it... " Suddenly it all came back: the cliff top fight, the pig of man falling to the rocks below, then -

"But," Jon backed to the bedroom window, he felt behind him on the sill and clutched at the strap of his camera where he had placed it the previous evening. "You're dead... this can't be happening..."

He wondered if this was a side effect of the hospital treatment he'd been forced to undergo. It wasn't so long past that he was strapped unwillingly into a bed. The demons he battled there were of his own making. Somehow this one felt more real. Maybe it was the smell, the sounds, something called out to him that this was no spectre of a sick mind. He looked at the pool of moisture beneath the abomination that used to be a human being and realised it was tangible.

"Oh no..." He whimpered. The monster took one more step into the room.

"I lay on those wet rocks for a long time before dying... I have that time to use now. Here. And it is plenty left to dispose of you..."

151

The young man suddenly swung the camera round and smashed it into the side of the creature's oozing, deformed head. As the bully reeled, Jon leapt past him, but not before a good portion of his own sleeve had been ripped from his arm by groping, slimy fingers. Once on the landing, Jon turned to face the mouldering Captain Millgard. A huge decaying fist came through the air at lightening speed and split his lip.

Jon was surprised and dismayed that his answering blow at the great beast's stomach had no effect. The officer's hands reached forward and closed round his opponent's weak shoulders. 'He's merely playing with me or I'd be dead by now,' thought Jon as his vision grew hazy. The cottage was so compact that it was hard to think of an escape route. It was hard to think at all. For all his planning, the delay had given the Captain time to act, and he was thrown down the stairs by his aggressor without a moment's hesitation.

*   *   *

"Something heavy just fell inside," said George, who had mustered up some courage and was peering in through the Kitchen window. "I think we should go in. The cottage isn't fighting back any more or we'd already be out on the road." Constable Geddes agreed. Moses wasn't so sure.

"That's devils' work afoot in there," he said firmly. "It's too far gone for us to get involved." As if to prove his point, the old man walked over to the other side of the road and seated himself on the verge amidst the cow parsley. He looked like an early arrival for a Victorian Melodrama. "It's too late for us to do anything other than watch it play out, no wonder old Jess didn't want to speak of it," he added, and folded his arms with a sour look on his face.

However, Constable Geddes thought differently. He looked across at Moses, then at George. He straightened his uniform.

"I think you're right. It is my duty to enter this cottage and make sure the occupants have come to no harm. It sounds like there's even more damage getting done, the least I can do is investigate it for the owner's sake." So saying, he walked up to the cottage, put one foot on the kitchen windowsill and hauled himself inside.

*　　　*　　　*

Mary leaned forward and tapped the sergeant's shoulder. He tensed visibly. Perhaps she was going to kill him. He should have radioed back to the station. His foot pushed the accelerator closer to the floor. Mary tapped his shoulder again.

"Excuse me, but you're going the wrong way," she said. "The cottage is down the road to the left. I remember it from when we came back from the supermarket."

"Yes, miss," he started to perspire. "This is a... short cut." They would soon be in the nearby town and at the nice, safe, police station. He didn't like dealing with mental disorders. Besides, there he would find back-up...

The heavy bulk of the most recent edition British road atlas turned his thoughts to a stunned darkness. The car slewed off the road as its driver fell unconscious onto the steering wheel.

*   *   *

The inhuman Captain waited at the top of the stairs.
He knew that Minton was only dazed. As soon as the
crumpled heap below moved, he would be upon him.
Then, as planned, he would break every little bone in
Minton's defenceless body. This threat was spoken out
loud, and Jon heard the words as he slipped into
wakefulness. He remained still, with his eyes closed
and his head throbbing. Waiting until his returning
strength would allow him to drag his aching body into
the kitchen. Then, perhaps, he could find a sharp knife.
That had been his plan. Banking on the Captain's
sluggish speed and desire to cause him pain Jonathan
hoped that the damage inflicted by the fall had not been
too great.

'Oh God, please give me strength. Please free
me from this nightmare. Got to get the police...' he
repeated over and over in his head, barely hearing the
threats being uttered above him. Tired with waiting for
some signs of life, the revolting monster began to
descend the stairs; this beast was slowly wringing every
drop of terror from Jon's soul... and from his bladder.
He had never been as frightened in his life. Frozen in
terror, he wondered if this is what it had felt like when
his poor fiancée had ploughed into the ground at a
hundred miles an hour... had she too been petrified,
cast into a statue of horror as the aeroplane lost
control...

*   *   *

Moving through the kitchen was like wading through honey. George and Constable Geddes' limbs felt like heavy rubber, and a curious dream-like quality attached itself to their surroundings. George put his hand on the constable's arm for stability.

"Listen," he said, and found himself shouting, as though in a high wind. "There's – someone – coming – down – stairs." It took a great effort to move his jaw and speak. Geddes forced himself through the turgid air, making imperceivable progress towards the kitchen door.

"Yes! I – hear – it – too! This – way!" He bellowed. The words fell flat; it was as if everything was being muffled. It was the deadening, otherworldly sound that you got after a heavy snowfall.

Moses sprang to his feet outside with surprising speed, staring in astonishment at the girl who ran down the lane towards him from the direction of the pub. Her nightdress was ripped and stained, she wore one slipper, and blood dripped from a cut in her neck. For all the world she looked as though she'd been in a car accident. What Moses didn't know was that the stream of black oily smoke just round the bend was from the very police car that the girl had just fought herself clear of.

She had a manic look in her eyes and he watched with fascination, barely recognising the woman from the photographs and from the meal at his own establishment not two days before. She moved towards the cottage, mumbling what sounded like a name. The old man could do nothing but gaze at her in wonder, and wish with all his heart that he had never heard the local legend of 'The Smuggler and the Revenue Officer' from his grandparents all those years earlier. He watched, in a torment of his own indecision, as the distraught woman disappeared. She jumped through the busted kitchen window to join his two comrades who were somewhere in the belly of the cottage. It was as if she was being sucked into the building.

*   *   *

Coming to his senses, Jon scrabbled along the short hallway towards the closed kitchen door on his hands and knees. He reached for the iron handle. Just as he touched it two things happened simultaneously. The vulgar hands of the officer gripped his left leg with vice-like strength, and the door swung open into the kitchen, pulled by a real human being on the other side.

*   *   *

Through the fug George spotted the small door leading out of the kitchen, and grabbed hold of the black metal mortice knob.

"Help me pull!" He cried to Geddes, but the constable had his hands full with a distraught woman who was wailing, trying to barge past them and reach the door herself.

"Keep away! Miss, you're not helping!" He said forcefully, trying to push her back towards the broken window. He grabbed her shoulders and tried to move her away from the door that had now swung open into the kitchen, revealing her injured husband on the hall floor, flailing around like a landed fish.

Upon seeing his beaten face she roared like a woman possessed, Geddes forced her back again with the palms of both his hands acting like a riot shield.

156

"Let us help him! You don't know who else is back there!" He pushed Mary with a little more force than he intended and she staggered, bumping into the wooden dining table. Her hand closed on a sturdy glass half-empty bottle of milk.

Ignoring the activity elsewhere in the house, the bloated abomination that had once been human, calmly and deliberately stood over Jonathan's body. Slowly, oh so slowly, the officer applied pressure to the young man's already broken leg. The pain increased, grating on every nerve until, with a sound like an egg breaking the bone snapped completely, shooting a wave of unbearable agony through Jon's entire being. He screamed, then fainted, unaware of the young shop assistant's hands that were wrapped around his own...

George pulled, God how he pulled! But he was tugging at two hundred years of revenge, and it was much too strong for him alone. He was gripping the man's wrists, and he heard a sharp snap as the demon began laughing. He heard the scream, but it sounded so distant that he didn't think it came from the man in front of him.

"Geddes," he cried, "for Christ's sake help me!" The policeman turned his head to glance at George, and in that instant Mary struck. She had thwarted the policeman in the car and she was damned if she would let anyone else stand between her and her husband.

Soured milk poured over Geddes' uniform in the split second before the inverted bottle crashed against the side of his head, knocking him cold and slashing his face. The force of the blow pushed him to the floor, the crazed wife stepped over his legs and grabbed at George. He had such a tight grip on Jonathan's hands that Mary ripped the shirt from his back, peeling it away from him as if it were made of paper.

The giant festering beast in the hallway set to work on Jonathan's other leg, releasing his hold when he noticed the commotion from the kitchen. His killing lust partly satiated, he decided to take some more companions with him on his journey back to the netherworld... The shock of Jonathan's body being suddenly set free, and the force of George pulling meant that the chemist's assistant was hurled backwards across the room. He cannoned into the wooden dresser, and as he fell forward, grabbed at a drawer handle to save himself. The drawer flew open, showering cutlery over the already messy floor. The young woman was oblivious to everything except the disgusting, malodorous thing in front of her.

Standing in the doorway was the sole object of Mary's hatred and fear. She launched herself at it, only to be smashed to one side, joining the litter of bodies on the red kitchen tiles. George looked up and couldn't believe the havoc that met his gaze! Mary Minton lay bunched up by the back door, an ugly mauve bruise beginning to swell on her cheek bone. Constable Geddes was beginning to come round from his head injury, gruesome scarlet trickles mapping his pallid face. In the internal doorway stood the massive frame of the revenue officer, dressed in what appeared to be a pantomime costume of the lowest quality.

He was panting like a sick dog trying to gasp for air, for his time on this plane was nearly up, and unfortunately for him Minton was still alive. Framed between the monster's legs, splayed out and groaning, Jonathan Minton wavered between pain-wracked awareness and the sweet vacancy of unconsciousness.

*   *   *

Moses Creddle had heard the shouting, had seen the girl, and had done nothing. Wavering with indecision. Now the sound of crashing cutlery spurred him to action. He moved across the road and stared in through the empty window casement. He saw young George slowly rising to his feet. He saw the huge ragged Law Man lumbering across the room. And he shouted.

"George! Look out, George lad!" The handle of a bread-saw was gripped tightly, and George wheeled round like a berserker, drawing the serrated knife across the Captain's throat. Thick dark-green blood sprayed out over the tattered remains of George's shirt. The giant foe fell dead, taken just before his time was up; killed before he'd finished off Jonathan Minton.

Outside the oak tree suddenly stopped swaying, and a horrible cracking sound came from deep down, as though a vast unholy hand was tearing it out by the roots. The old trunk was breaking. Moses Creddle noticed it and yelled at George to run deeper into the cottage. Geddes was wandering around the kitchen, dazed, not knowing where he was, or what he was doing. George ignored Moses' instructions and steered him towards the window, pushing him out through the battered hole into the daylight.

He was just about to return for the newly-weds when Moses caught him and used all his strength to pull the young man backwards away from the sill.

"Get away, get away!" The landlord was saying. "The tree's going to fall any second now!" He pushed the constable out into the road. George tugged at the old man's sleeve, and pointed back at the cottage.

"There's still two people in there... I must..." With a splintering of long dead wood, the huge oak keeled over onto the front of the cottage.

How are the mighty fallen. Down came the heavy tree, splitting smoke-blackened beams, smashing ancient hewn timber like matchwood, crushing age-old

159

bricks, and powdering whitewashed plaster into a fine dust. The chimney fell in with a roar, and the whole cottage was demolished as surely as if a bomb had been planted beneath it. Every wall, beam, floor, roof tile, window, ceiling and piece of furniture collapsed inward with a sickening rumble onto the three prostrate forms in the kitchen. A huge bloom of dust swept across the road, slowly obscuring the injured policeman, the disbelieving face of the chemist's assistant, and the lined, sorrowing features of the old man.

THE FLYING MACHINE

He knew already what it was like to travel rapidly through the air. There had been that unforgettable – *unfortunate* – occasion when, surrounded on three sides by heavily armed opponents and a cliff at his back, he'd turned and flung himself out into the sky above the lake. There was no hesitation.

He had been intrigued, in a strangely dispassionate way, as to how quickly, yet with no sense of time, he'd hurtled towards the black surface which glowed dully like polished steel. How at the last minute he'd straightened his body by some ancient instinct so that he almost slid into the icy water feet first. The cold had stunned him more than the impact and he swore afterwards – though privately doubted – that his feet had touched the very bottom of the lake.

But this was different. A drop of one hundred and fifty feet in the manner of a falling rock was nothing compared to rising like a bird. Having the chance to look down on a world that didn't approach you at the speed of an arrow. As soon as your stomach caught up with you, that is, and once you could put the feeling to the back of your mind that any minute this flimsy contraption of wood, string, and skins would tumble out of the sky. It was hard not to imagine the components prising apart, allowing the machine to spread itself widely, and permanently, on the ground below... But it could be done. You just had to concentrate.

Direction was another problem. On the ground, to make the wheels go where he had wanted them on the long downward slope to the cliff, he had attached steering reins from a horse bridle. Up here in the air any violent tugging that involved him moving more than his arms and head set the whole machine wobbling alarmingly! He didn't fancy a death dive just at that moment. So, for now, he tried to relax and lose himself in the thrill of doing and seeing things that no man had ever attempted before. It was a miracle.

The day was fine, balmy even. Spring greened the land below, the ever nearing sky was a deeper blue than he could have imagined. The wind seemed light. In this hill country there were strong thermals, currents of air that neither he, nor any of his fellow human beings had heard of, or considered. On these invisible jets he soared even higher, spiralling, but moving steadily away from his take off point: that cliff where, after bumping down the long sweep of tussocky grass at a frightening speed, he had shot off the edge into infinity. A sickening dive followed by a stomach wrenching jerk and he was climbing, the lake below just a large black birthmark on the surrounding countryside.

What a weapon this could be! This wonderful machine! What a way to watch enemy troop movements from above. How marvellous it would be to carry stones into the sky and drop them on soldiers powerless to defend themselves from the menace of the air. Why stop there? If attacking troops could be spotted, why not go higher and see their military camps; drop rocks on them before they even left their tents! Increase the altitude still further and you could view other lands, see warring kingdoms, send assassins into those places and kill off the leaders before the battles even started. Fly soldiers into other countries and invade without the hazards of sea travel. No more sick men, green and listless after a rough crossing, trying to establish a beachhead against ready armies... Simply swoop down on them and attack from behind. All manner of warfare could be revolutionised. Thanks to him and his flying machine anyone could become ruler of the entire world... Once he had found a way to steer the thing.

He had already discovered, by a heart stopping system of trial and error, how to make the flying machine go down. If he leaned forward the nose would dip and a lurch in his bowels would tell him that he was dropping fast. Lean back and he would level out and eventually climb again in those gently relaxing gyres. Steering... yes, that would be a possible problem, but he already had fresh ideas...

As pine forests passed beneath him like rough olive deerskins he reasoned that if a boat could change direction whilst travelling through water by turning a rudder – or jabbing a sweep oar into the line of flow – then why not the same thing for a flying machine? A rudder on top, either behind or in front of the sail would... yes, the sail!

Gingerly he turned and managed to unstep the small mast. The sail had been added to give the machine greater speed, but the spiralling movement implied that he was permanently tacking, sailing into the wind. With a resigned sigh he let the mast drop over the side, quickly falling to the hazy fields below. Relieved of the weight and obstruction, the contrivance made a sudden sweep upwards that took his breath away!

Peering down he could see the sail of rough woollen cloth rippling and fluttering as it dwindled to a pale brown dot against the dark green trees, and then it disappeared completely. He gulped, a little nervously. Heavens, he was really high up... So high, it seemed, that there was less air. He found himself taking deeper breaths, and continually yawning without feeling tired. It was becoming *very* cold. How could it be so, with the sky so clear and blue... and the warm sun still visible?

The distant mountains were now not so distant. What had appeared smooth, snow painted, slopes when viewed from the lakeside revealed themselves as many jagged peaks and passes, deep gorges, secret icy valleys. Time to look for a suitable landing place, for he couldn't turn back. He must by now be a good day's walk from the lake and the village... The lake!

Where had it gone? He turned his head and neck without moving his arms, surely not that tiny black dot far behind that suddenly flashed in the afternoon sun... He tried to twist round to get his bearings, but that set the contraption rocking violently. So he set himself the now urgent task of finding somewhere to set down. He had food for three days at a stretch, but he was already a long way over country unexplored by his clan. Who knew what dangers lurked beneath the close-growing pines, or lay in wait behind the large grey blisters of rock that punctured the skin of the forest. An expanse of grass as flat as possible was what he required.

After a short time scouting he would have settled for a patch of soft heather, or a deep pool that he could plunge into. He didn't actually have to keep the flying machine, he knew it intimately: every tie, strut, piece of leather had been lovingly constructed over a period of three moons. The others hadn't known what he was up to. They would only scoff, as they had done so often in the past. Let them find out when he could show them a path to victory over all the other clans! Then his pride and joy wouldn't be just *a* flying machine; it would be *the* flying machine. They would probably name it after him; his name would be praised evermore as the 'Great Inventor'.

A sudden awareness of the cold brought him out of his revelry. He had been prepared for a certain drop in temperature (why else did birds have a thick layer of feathers), but this was a bitter midwinter chill. Glancing up, he saw that the highest peak was much closer, and that he was no longer looking up at it. He was level with the blindingly bright cone of snow that marked the summit! White-clad rocks were below him now. No wonder the temperature had dropped!

A thrill coursed through him. He was going to travel *over* the mountains. No one knew what lay the other side of the... The flying machine gave a sudden lurch and started to corkscrew rapidly down into a fold in the land. Panicking, he leaned back to try and increase his height, but here above the snow field he'd lost the warm air thermals of the lower slopes. There was no response. The ground whirled closer and closer, and he found himself spinning down into a deep, wide, gorge carved by some ancient ice flow between two sheer rock walls.

At the last moment his erratic flight levelled out so that he was flying straight along the valley, but still rapidly losing height. When it came the terrible landing was much heavier and faster than he would have expected. The machine stopped dead, caught in one of the obstructions which were unseen from above. Many similar obstacles carpeted the ground in a loose, but perilous, gauntlet.

In seconds the once graceful beast of a machine converted itself into nothing but splintered firewood. Yet he himself seemed relatively unharmed. A couple of bruises, a long shallow scratch across his face, a slight feeling of nausea, and he was standing in the scattered snow, surveying the incredible mess about him.

For a few minutes he felt incredibly warm; relief sweated on his brow, and the snowfield was several degrees milder than the air above. But there was a chill breeze, and the sun did not penetrate to the depths of the valley floor. He shivered. Groping around in the wreckage he found his provision bag. Resisting the temptation to begin eating – for he suddenly felt ravenous – he sat back unsteadily on his haunches, and tried to think clearly as to what he should do next. He found it difficult to concentrate, and he had to continually take huge gulps of air to try and clear his mind. It almost felt as though the valley was cut off from the atmosphere outside, the air seemed so thin...

A long hard journey was ahead of him there was no doubt, but where was he in relation to his starting point, and in what direction should he set off was left to ponder. He knew that he hadn't crossed over the highest peak, but what if he had been blown round it, so he was now on the wrong side of the mountain? One thing was paramount: if he was to stay alive he must get off this snowfield as quickly as possible. Or find some means of warming himself...

Many thousands of feet below late spring kissed the forests and valleys, up here winter could last for nine moons of the year. He needed warmth; he needed food, he needed sleep, yet to close his heavy eyelids in these temperatures he knew would be fatal. Thus one of the crumpled wings of the flying machine caught his eye. Deerskins! Why not? They were no use for anything else, and he had a plentiful supply. A few swift blows with his knife gave him three decent sized hides. He wrapped them around his shivering body, greedily ate a couple of oatcakes from his meal bag, then slept.

*　　　*　　　*

When he awoke it was light, but he had the accurate impression that he had slept for many hours, and that this was early the following morning. At least he was warm, but the atmosphere seemed no less rarefied. He yearned for a good lungful of air like an alcoholic craving his next drink. Yawning, he stretched in his improvised sleeping bag, and the outer skin crackled icily. He reached up and dragged his fingers through frost rimmed hair. Relieved that he was suffering no aches and pains other than a general stiffness, he crawled out to survey the day.

The cold bit into his body and he hurriedly snatched an inner deer skin. Wrapping it around himself like a cloak, he scrutinised his landing site in more detail. The floor of the valley appeared very uneven, and was apparently covered in a layer of branches, as though someone had been gathering firewood and had spread it out to dry before the snows came. Perhaps, years ago, this ravine had been sheltered enough to sustain some trees. When the climate changed, as it sometimes did for several years, the forest had died and fallen here.

There was no possibility of climbing out of the gorge. The cliff walls rose sheer for fifty feet on either side. He observed that the valley floor sloped gradually upwards for about a quarter of a mile so that it levelled with the side of the mountain. There lay his route to the outside world. Without hesitation he shouldered his meal bag and struck out in that direction.

It was not easy. Sticks, branches and debris covered the whole area. There were no paths, and it took him several hours to negotiate the spiky obstacles, natural barriers that almost seemed to be trying to keep him confined to that desolate place. His shortness of breath forced him to rest every few yards. As he tripped, jumped and climbed across this snow laden devastation he had a strange feeling that he should be paying more attention to this nightmare landscape than he actually was. He could see why the trees had died. If the remains of their leaves were anything to go by they were of a very temperate variety. Some of the tattered foliage flapping in the icy breeze seemed monstrously large. He felt some; it was thick, almost like leather...

Finally he had done it. The ravine fell below and behind him, and he could now see where he was. Disappointment washed over him. Instead of reaching the side of a mountain with a view back down to forest lands he found himself on another snow field at least a mile wide! It cut off any view downwards. However, turning and looking up he could see the looming bulk of the great peak that yesterday he thought he might fly over. White powdered snow steamed in a windblown cloud against the fierce blue sky. It seemed tantalisingly near... Surely only a couple of hours walking would take him to the summit, and from there he would be able to see... What?

Nothing, if his vision kept blurring, and if distant objects continued to swirl around like fish in a stream. Deep breathing helped steady his sight slightly. From the crest he would be able to see *the whole world*, that's if the legends about the mountain were to be believed. Perhaps there would be more friendly terrain on the other side that he could reach quickly? Low country where he would be able to breathe again. Also the snowfield was beginning to hypnotise him with its startling beauty.

At diminishing intervals he felt that he could just sit down and look at it for ever, turning into one of those frozen boulders... but the tingling in his face and hands kept reminding him that to succumb to that urge would mean certain death. Pausing yet again for ragged breath...where had the air gone? Why was he panting? Perhaps it was the cold; perhaps air was heavy and he was too high up – after all when the wind blew it created a pressure against you, thus implying that air was an object, and all objects had weight... Now he was rambling; his mind was going on little journeys of its own. He tried to dismiss it and concentrate on the job in hand. Imagination stimulated by unforeseen circumstances and new exhilarating vistas.

Squatting down once more, he reached into his meal bag and... it was empty! Surely not. He'd hardly touched it. Inspection showed him the several rips and tears acquired while climbing over the wreckage of the forest. Despair momentarily gripped his heart. He could never go back and search for the food. It might be anywhere, and he would just waste his failing strength. No. He should be able to last several days without eating, and he could fill his stomach with snow. As long as he could get out of the cold wind he should be alright.

With a deep sigh that produced the effect of a fire breathing dragon venting its wrath in clouds of smoke, he turned and struck upwards. He was thankful that there were no more twisted boughs to climb over, and that the slope wasn't too steep.

*   *   *

Half a day later his hope was fading. The mountain was behaving in that way common to all such hills. When he reached the summit he found it was only a secondary, and lower, crest, so he climbed still higher. Gasping for breath, his head spinning, his exertions produced in him a prodigious sweat, and he shed the deerskins as being too cumbersome.

The light had changed slowly during the day from an eye-aching white to an equally dazzling yellow, and now, as he scaled what must *surely be* the last peak, the sky was suffused with a deep orange that heralded the treacherous chill of evening as his strength waned. By the Gods! It was the top! Yet there was no dramatic peak... The summit of the great mountain was flat. It seemed about thirty feet square to his tired eyes and... he rubbed them, staring in disbelief... What was this, a vision brought about by his ailing condition? There was someone there; a fellow human being! Perhaps he would have food and warm clothing!

"I have been expecting you," said the old man, rising from an ancient-looking chair, ornately carved and black with age. But was it merely a chair? The wood, glowing in the late sun, seemed far more intricate than any throne that he had seen in a chieftain's long house. The old man, too, had an air of easy authority. This was accentuated by the long grey robes of a sage. He wore no thick furs or skins, and indeed didn't require them. It was noticeable that this quiet place was as warm as a summer day in the forest.

"Expecting me?" asked the adventurous man, slowly relaxing in the heat, and feeling the tired stiffness ebb away from his muscles, "but how? Where exactly am I? And more to the point, who are you?"

"I don't need to tell you who I am. Deep inside you you know the answer to that question. Where you are, I should have thought obvious. You are on the top of the world, just as you wished. Now, take rest in that chair." He did so, glad to lower his tired limbs into such a well crafted seat. Almost immediately he was aware of a steady movement. The chair was revolving, very slowly, on its own axis.

"Notice how you turn just as the world turns... You can see everything... Forests, mountains, seas, deserts, plains, farmlands, continents, islands, these are all within your sight, and within reach of your beckoning."

"From here..." murmured the man with a contented sigh, "You could rule the entire world."

"No. Never rule," the old countered. "*Influence.* I can *influence* things. It is within my power to guide things, but only for the good of the universe." The man surveyed a world that was now bathed in the red rays of an enormous setting sun, split by a couple of thin black cloud lines; a sun far larger than he had ever viewed from down in his own valley, with a shimmering outline in the heat haze rising from the warm lands below.

"So did... Did you guide me here?" he asked hesitantly.

"I may have had *some* influence; but no, you came of your own accord... like all the others in their flying machines." He paused, to allow the words to sink into the man's tired mind.

"What others?" the man leapt to his feet.

"All the others who did things for the wrong reasons. Every few years someone manages to harness the power of flight, but always they think of their own physical might. They want to use the marvellous invention as a terror, a weapon against their fellow men. I cannot allow this. Until man flies for the sake of enjoyment alone all flights will end here. Yours was relatively short. Some come from far distant lands... but, they all end up in that valley down on the mountainside. That way no one will ever find them." The man collapsed back into the chair.

"But... I don't understand. You mean they all crash in the dead forest?"

"I know of no forest? Your wooden bird fell where all the others fell. There is no forest there, just a graveyard of flying machines, from all eras, from all countries, from all men... and it is the resting place for many of their pilots. You proved very resourceful by leaving the valley."

Amazement and anger welled up in the adventurous man. Who was this old fool to decide what other men should and shouldn't do! It was short lived. His soul admitted the answer, and with this his whole being sagged, tired, dispirited, ready to accept the inevitable.

"Why was *I* not killed in the crash? My machine was smashed to pieces."

"I will have no one die unnecessarily. Many of the others died on the long flight here, the air and the cold both played their part. I could not help them." Relief flooded his mind. That surely meant that the old man *would* help him. It was just the machine he had wanted destroyed... along with all those other hundreds – thousands – of flying machines going back into the mists of time.

He saw what it was. The old man smashed the inventions, but sent the creators back to work for peace, and to steer other people away from similar warlike ideas. A noble gesture.

"How do I get down from here?" he asked, knowing now that the old man could do anything he wished. A smile crossed the brown, leathery face of his companion.

"You fly," he said gently.

"But my machine is - "

"No. *You* fly." The adventurous man licked his dry lips and pondered the suggestion.

"It is within your power to grant me that then?"

"I can influence the elements to allow it to take place if you so wish. Yes."

A delicious shiver of anticipation coursed the man's body.

"W-what do I do? How do I begin?" The old man extended his hand, and pointed westward.

"You face the globe of the setting sun, on that edge of the plateau..." The excited man did as he was instructed, and saw below him all the world in microcosm: trees, lakes, rivers, farms, and beyond it all the black outline of the coast, fingers of land reaching into a sun-burnished sea, coppered and mysterious. Far far away, on an indistinct horizon, where the red disc touched the water, his eyes could just discern the shape of islands, dark and intriguing. As he gazed, a long line of large birds flapped overhead, followed by several other ranks; flying solemnly out towards the ocean and the setting sun; seeking new horizons on their migration.

"I wish I could go with them..." he said, mainly to himself. The old man studied him. "Flying with them would be to some real purpose. They can explore much further than me. They are going to places where my machine would never have reached."

"I told you," said the old man, quietly, "I can allow you to fly. Stand still where you are, and spread your arms. Soon you will be with the birds, and you will have your heart's true desire." The expectant pilot stood right on the edge of the plateau, and looked straight at the sun. Strangely it didn't hurt his eyes, he no longer needed to squint against the rays. He felt the rock beneath his feet and flattened his toes against the earth. Taking a deep breath he spread his arms wide.

"Now jump," said the old man, it was a whisper, like a gust of wind caressing his cheek.

He threw himself out into the open space, trying almost to dive into the red fire of the sky. There was a sensation of rushing down, down, down at a great speed. Then a terrific jerk that plunged him into blackness, followed by a weightlessness that filled his whole being.

His spirit rose to join the birds, and he soared with them on trade-winds of pure joy, reaching out for the oceanic island chain.

The old man allowed himself another smile, then returned to his chair to wait once again.